Vixen

Also From Rebecca Zanetti

DARK PROTECTORS
Fated
Claimed
Tempted
Hunted
Consumed
Provoked
Twisted
Shadowed
Tamed
Marked
Teased
Tricked
Tangled
Talen
Vampire's Faith
Demon's Mercy
Alpha's Promise
Hero's Haven
Guardian's Grace

THE ANNA ALBERTINI FILES
Disorderly Conduct
Bailed Out

DEEP OPS
Hidden
Taken
Fallen
Shaken
Broken

REALM ENFORCERS
Wicked Ride
Wicked Edge

Wicked Burn
Wicked Kiss
Wicked Bite

SCORPIUS SYNDROME SERIES
Scorpius Rising
Blaze Erupting
Mercury Striking
Shadow Falling
Justice Ascending
Storm Gathering
Winter Igniting
Knight Awakening

SIN BROTHERS
Forgotten Sins
Sweet Revenge
Blind Faith
Total Surrender

BLOOD BROTHERS
Deadly Silence
Lethal Lies
Twisted Truths

MAVERICK MONTANA SERIES
Against the Wall
Under the Covers
Rising Assets
Over the Top

Vixen

A Dark Protectors/Rebels Novella

By Rebecca Zanetti

1001 DARK NIGHTS
PRESS

Vixen
A Dark Protectors/Rebels Novella
By Rebecca Zanetti

Copyright 2020 Rebecca Zanetti
ISBN: 978-1-970077-67-4

Foreword: Copyright 2014 M. J. Rose

Published by 1001 Dark Nights Press, an imprint of Evil Eye Concepts, Incorporated

Acknowledgments from the Author

A huge thank you to Liz Berry, MJ Rose, and Jillian Stein for banding together this amazing group of authors who have become such good friends. It's nice to know that we're not alone with all of the voices and characters in our heads. 2020 hasn't been the year we all hoped it would be, across the world, but we've had each other to text, call, and Zoom, and I think that has made a difference for so many of us.

Thanks also to the entire 1001 Dark Night team: Kimberly Guidroz, Kasi Alexander, Asha Hossain, and Jenn Watson from Social Butterfly. Also thanks to Anissa Beatty and the entire FB Rebecca's Rebels Street Team for the support!

Finally, a huge thank you to my family, Big Tone, Gabe, and Karlina for the support and laughs. I love you three.

Sign up for the 1001 Dark Nights Newsletter
and be entered to win a Tiffany Key necklace.

There's a contest every month!

Go to www.1001DarkNights.com to subscribe.

**As a bonus, all subscribers can download
FIVE FREE exclusive books!**

One Thousand and One Dark Nights

Once upon a time, in the future…

*I was a student fascinated with stories and learning.
I studied philosophy, poetry, history, the occult, and
the art and science of love and magic. I had a vast
library at my father's home and collected thousands
of volumes of fantastic tales.*

*I learned all about ancient races and bygone
times. About myths and legends and dreams of all
people through the millennium. And the more I read
the stronger my imagination grew until I discovered
that I was able to travel into the stories... to actually
become part of them.*

*I wish I could say that I listened to my teacher
and respected my gift, as I ought to have. If I had, I
would not be telling you this tale now.
But I was foolhardy and confused, showing off
with bravery.*

*One afternoon, curious about the myth of the
Arabian Nights, I traveled back to ancient Persia to
see for myself if it was true that every day Shahryar
(Persian: شهریار, "king") married a new virgin, and then
sent yesterday's wife to be beheaded. It was written
and I had read that by the time he met Scheherazade,
the vizier's daughter, he'd killed one thousand
women.*

Something went wrong with my efforts. I arrived in the midst of the story and somehow exchanged places with Scheherazade — a phenomena that had never occurred before and that still to this day, I cannot explain.

Now I am trapped in that ancient past. I have taken on Scheherazade's life and the only way I can protect myself and stay alive is to do what she did to protect herself and stay alive.

Every night the King calls for me and listens as I spin tales. And when the evening ends and dawn breaks, I stop at a point that leaves him breathless and yearning for more. And so the King spares my life for one more day, so that he might hear the rest of my dark tale.

As soon as I finish a story... I begin a new one... like the one that you, dear reader, have before you now.

Chapter 1

Robbing a bank shouldn't take this much work.

Especially since said bank was in the middle of a podunk town in the middle of freaking nowhere. Tabitha Rusko stepped out of her souped-up BMW and into the darkness of night, having waited too many days for a cloudy evening. The moon over this part of the world was often over-bright, and it had taken forever for stormy weather to finally arrive.

As a demonness, she should be able to control the weather, darn it. Thunder growled across the sky as if in perfect agreement.

She tugged a black rope from the back seat and shut her door, winding the heavy nylon around her shoulder. Then she fetched the grappling hook from the trunk along with the compact drill.

This was ridiculous.

She took a deep breath and ran across the quiet street toward the silent building.

"Going somewhere?" a deep voice asked.

She jumped and bit back a yelp, swinging around to make out a figure leaning against a maple tree by the front door of the bank. Oh, crap. "Detective O'Connell," she breathed, her heartbeat ramming into a cadence that might kill her. "What are you doing here?" There was no way he'd followed her, because she'd driven all over the town to make sure she was clear. This was a bank robbery, for Pete's sake.

He pushed off from the tree, striding in the casual lope that screamed bad boy sexy—even for a human. "I had the oddest feeling you were up to something after seeing you drive by this bank so many times the last week, and considering you desperately want the recording I have secured inside, I went with my instincts." He reached her, and his unique scent of smoked honey wafted her way.

That smell had chased her through dreams until she could finally identify it. Why it was so blatantly masculine, she'd never understand. "You've been watching me? Stalking me?" When all else fails, attack.

"No. My office is just down the street," he said, his tone dry. He wore a dark T-shirt and faded jeans with a gun strapped to his thigh and a badge at his belt. He was about six-two with thick brown hair, matching beard, and blue eyes that seemed to see through her without much effort.

If she didn't know better, she'd think he was something beyond human. But he wasn't. Even now, she could sense the illness in him. One he thought he could hide. Yet another thing that had kept her up at night. "I'm not doing anything wrong."

He looked down at her rope, drill, and grappling hook. "Attempted robbery of a bank is a felony."

"I haven't attempted anything." She kept her feet on the sidewalk. "I'm not even on the bank's property." Yet. Of course, the cop knew that fact. Why had he stopped her before she'd at least trespassed? He seemed to rescue everyone, or rather, every woman around who needed help. "Do you keep a bunch of dogs and cats, too?" she blurted before she could help herself.

He cocked his head to the side. "Two dogs and no cats. Okay, one cat, but he just stops by when the weather is bad or he's really hungry." Evan stuck his hand in his jeans pocket. "Maybe two cats."

The guy was a natural rescuer. Also a pain in the butt. "If you're such a great guy, why won't you give me that recording you have of me?" She fluttered her eyelashes in an age-old move.

He sighed and took her arm, his grip firm. "I promise you'll get the video the second you graduate from anger management. You have to understand that you could've killed those guys, and while they probably deserved it for harassing you, I can't just let you off the hook. You do seem to have anger issues."

Oh, he had no idea. She'd been innocently minding her own business and the punks had accosted her, so she'd kicked their butts. It was too bad the whole situation had been caught on camera, and since one of the kids was the sheriff's son, she had been charged. Evan had helped her, though. She dug in her heels and stopped them both.

He stiffened and turned to face her. "How are you so strong?" Releasing her, he rubbed the back of his neck. "Or maybe I've just lost my strength." He sighed, his broad chest moving with the effort. "What was your plan tonight?" He sounded merely curious.

She couldn't tell him, and she really had to get a move on. "I'm really sorry about this," she whispered, setting her stance and turning more fully to face him.

He shook his head. "That isn't an answer."

"No, but this is." She lowered her chin and attacked his mind, sending enough power to knock him out and scramble his brain enough that he wouldn't remember the evening.

He cocked his head to the side. "What is?"

Her mouth dropped open. She'd sent enough pain his way that he should've dropped to the pavement instantly. Was there something wrong with her? All demons could attack minds—it was one of their strongest skills. While she was only twenty-five years old, she'd learned how in her early teens. She should be able to kill the guy with the right force.

Yet there he stood.

She tried again, this time holding nothing back.

His chin lowered. "What the hell are you doing?"

"Did you feel that?" she whispered. Tingles exploded throughout her abdomen.

He stepped closer. "Feel what?"

Oh, crap. Her powers were gone. How the heck had that happened? "This town is bad luck," she yelled, throwing her hands up and knocking him beneath the chin with the drill.

He snatched it from her hand. "Ouch."

"*That* hurt you?" she yelled, fury ripping through her with the force of a real demon mind attack. One that actually worked. "You should be slobbering all over the pavement right now."

The clouds parted, and the moon beamed down, highlighting the angles of his rugged face. His beyond blue eyes laser focused on her. "Are you all right? Maybe we should get you to a professional or something."

Yeah, she probably did sound like a lunatic.

Evan stiffened and then partially turned toward the street.

The air grew heavy, and Tabi sighed, her stomach dropping as a demon strolled their way from the shadows. "This day just couldn't get any worse," she muttered. "Evan? You might want to run now."

* * * *

Evan shifted his weight to put the blonde pain-in-the-ass behind him while he faced the threat. There was no doubt the man heading toward them, body relaxed, eyes intense…was a threat. He would've known that even if Tabitha hadn't just told him to run. "What kind of trouble are you in, darlin'?" he asked, resting his hand on the butt of his gun.

Her sigh stirred the air around them. "The kind you wouldn't understand. Please leave, and I'll handle this."

He almost grinned. The woman was frighteningly petite with long blonde hair and the deepest black eyes he'd ever seen. While she looked fragile, she moved with a power and confidence that had intrigued him from the first time he'd arrested her. Yet there was no way she could fight the guy headed their way. Although Evan wasn't at his best right now, either. If this current weakness in his limbs continued, he'd have to give notice at the department. But not tonight or until he solved the murder of the dirtbag Monte Loften. Tonight, he was helping Tabi.

The guy finally arrived and stopped walking a couple of feet away. "Hello, Tabitha."

So they did know each other. Evan cocked his head. "Care to introduce us?" His adrenaline flowed through his veins, and he sank into the sensation for the briefest of seconds. He missed feeling strong and healthy.

Tabi stepped to his side. "Detective O'Connell, this is Richard Goncharov. He is now leaving."

Had her voice trembled? Evan studied the newcomer as he was studied right back. Tall and broad, Evan wasn't accustomed to looking up at anybody. This guy was about six-foot-seven with dark eyes and thick blonde hair almost as light as Tabi's. Were they related? "Your brother?" Evan asked.

Richard smiled, revealing strong white teeth. "Her betrothed."

Betrothed? Oh, hell no. Evan snorted. "What century are you from?"

The smile widened. "You wouldn't believe me if I told you."

What was going on with these people? "Tabi?" Evan asked.

"It's a long story." She elbowed him in the ribs and settled her feet next to him. "But we haven't done anything wrong, so please let us be, Detective."

No way was Evan leaving her with this guy. While he might not understand what was going on, his instincts had never failed him. "Actually, you're both skulking near the bank, and I can take you in briefly for questioning." Which might be a good idea.

Richard stared down at Tabi. "Is this guy for real?"

She exhaled. "Yes."

Richard lifted his nose, sniffing the air. He paused and studied Evan with even more intensity. "You're dying."

Evan jolted and then regained control. How the hell did he know that? "Excuse me?"

"Leave him alone." Tabi pushed forward with the nylon rope still around her shoulder and a grappling hook in her left hand. "Let's go, Richard. We can fight about our future and leave the detective be. I won't allow him to be hurt."

"The mere fact that you don't want him harmed makes me want to harm him," Richard said slowly.

What the fuck? Evan shoved Tabi behind him again and tossed the drill to the ground. "That was a threat against a law enforcement officer." Well, kind of. Either way, he could get this guy away from Tabi and run a background check on him for crimes. "You're coming with me."

"I'm bored." Richard lowered his chin in the same way Tabi had earlier. "Say goodbye to your brain." He focused hard on Evan's face.

"That's it." Evan reached for the cuffs in his back pocket.

Richard stepped back. "What the hell?"

Tabi hopped back to Evan's side. "Oh, thank goodness. I thought it was me. I'm fine. You couldn't attack his mind, either?"

Okay. They were both nuts. "I think we should get you two some help." Evan set the cuffs back in place and reached for his phone. "We have a nice and secured area at the hospital where we can figure out what's going on." Was Tabi involved in some type of weird cult with this moron? It figured that a crazy blonde would make him wish he could live longer. The fact that she was nuts should diminish his desire for her. Nope. Maybe the shrink from anger management could help her.

"You really should leave," Tabi said, her gaze remaining on Richard. "I mean it, Richard. Don't hurt him."

Enough. Evan reached for his gun, stopping when Tabi cried out. Tears leaked from her eyes and her body shook. "Tabi?"

Her chin firmed and she snapped her head up. Her legs visibly trembled, and the air thickened around her. She coughed and then sucked in a breath. "You attacked me?" she all but growled at Richard.

He smiled. "Just wanted to make sure I still had it." Then he lowered his chin again, and his eyes gleamed in the darkness.

Fury lit her face. "Don't you ever—" She cried out again and dropped the grappling hook. It bounced near the discarded drill.

Evan instinctively reached for her arm. "Tabi?"

She jerked and then settled, taking a deep breath. Slowly, she turned her head to face him. "How did you do that?"

"Do what?" Evan didn't like how pale she'd become, so he gentled his grip on her. What the hell was going on here?

"You, um, stopped the mind attack," she breathed, her eyes wide.

Heat flowed through him. "Honey? I think you need help." How had the jackass in front of him convinced the woman that her mind could be attacked? "Let's get you to the hospital, and I'll take a complete report from you about whatever you're involved in. I am going to help you." While he'd sensed she was in some sort of trouble, he hadn't figured on anything this crazy. It'd be nice to take down a cult before he died, if that's what was going on.

His own headache was about to drop him to the ground, but he was used to that. In fact, if his head stopped hurting, he'd know he was close to death. Not that it wasn't coming for him, anyway.

Tabi slipped her hand in his. "Let's get out of here."

The sweetness of her gesture dug into his chest and took hold. "How about we all go to the station?"

Richard's lips thinned, and he stared at their joined hands. "I guess I can wait for your disease to kill you, human." His eyes sparked again. "Your deadline is Thursday, Tabitha. Take me, or take death. Your choice." He turned and strode away.

Evan stiffened and reached for his gun.

"No," Tabi said softly. "Let him go. You know he didn't break any laws."

True. Evan wouldn't be able to hold him for long. "What's going on?" he asked quietly.

She shook her head. "I don't really know, to be honest." Then she looked up at him, her gaze earnest. "I have to go home now. We can talk after the anger management class tomorrow. I'm sure you'll be there to make sure I go."

"Let me help you." He could just take her in, but at the moment, he didn't have enough to really hold her on. Part of that was his fault in that he'd stopped her before she could use the rope and hook. His time was limited, and saving her had become his focus two weeks ago.

He hadn't figured out why.

Yet.

Chapter 2

Tabitha paced in the kitchen of her rental bungalow—or what counted as a bungalow in this small town. Yeah, it was charming and she loved it, but there was no chance she'd be able to stay. If Richard had found her, the Popovs wouldn't be far behind. She looked at the clock, knowing it was way too late to call. Yet she picked up her phone and pressed speed dial.

"Somebody better be dead," a grumpy voice answered.

Then a soft female voice in the background. "Who would call this late in the night?"

Tabi winced. "I'm so sorry to bother you, Raine. I didn't realize you had company." The deadly vampire-demon hybrid could probably pick up a woman with a lift of his dark eyebrow. He was more vampire than demon by far. Hence the charm.

Blankets rustled, and Raine chuckled. "No worries. Did you manage to rob the bank?"

"No." Tabitha leaned against the counter, wondering at her sanity in calling the vampire. Sure, they were stuck in this town together, and he was one of the only immortals around, but they weren't exactly friends. Not that she had friends or family or pretty much anybody. "I didn't know who else to call."

A door shut and then the sound of water pouring into a kettle came over the line. "I can help you rob the bank tomorrow night, if you'd like."

She was a demonness, for goodness' sakes. One who shouldn't need anybody's help to rob a darn bank. "No. I, ah, have a couple of questions." While she'd only been alive a quarter of a century, Raine had lived at least three hundred years, if not four.

"Okay." His low voice rumbled through the line. "Fire away."

She pushed aside warning, having to trust somebody. "Have you heard of humans who can block a demon mind attack?"

Quiet came over the line. "Why? Did somebody block your attack?"

She bit her lip, not wanting to put Evan in Raine's cross-hairs any more than was necessary. "Can we just go on hypotheticals here?"

Raine sighed. "I'm not fond of playing games, demonness, but I'll go along with you for now. The answer is that there are some enhanced human females—a very few—who were known as demon destroyers because they could block attacks. In fact, I believe that Kane Kayrs mated one. Yes. That's right. He did."

Kane Kayrs? He was one of the Kayrs brothers who ruled the Realm, which was a coalition of immortal species. "You're not a member of the Realm, are you?" It'd be nice to talk to Kane's mate, but Tabi didn't know anybody in the Realm.

"Ha," Raine snorted. "No. The Maxwell clan out of Montana has never aligned with anybody. My brothers would cut off my head if I even thought about it, and I'd probably let them do it."

"What's wrong with the Realm?" Tabi asked.

"It's easier not being a part of any coalition," Raine said easily. "Your family isn't aligned with the Realm, if I remember right."

She sighed. "I'm the only one left in my family. Didn't you know that?"

He paused. "No. The Ruskos have a reputation of being secretive and, frankly, nuts. I hadn't realized you were the only one left. No family at all?"

She sighed. "No. My parents died in the last dustup between immortals, and I was left with a nanny, who raised me. A human nanny."

Raine sucked in air—loudly. "You were raised by a human?"

Tabi opened her fridge for a bottle of wine. "Yep. She was kind and I loved her. She also knew all about the immortal world, so I'm well versed in whatever she knew. But we stayed off the grid mainly." Until last year, when everything had gone to crap. Tabi didn't need to share that with Raine. She liked the guy, but even she knew not to trust the Maxwells from Montana.

"Interesting. Well, if you have found a demon destroyer, keep her identity to yourself, if you don't choose to kill her." A kettle whistled loudly. "Most demons are fine with killing anybody who poses a threat to them, which is probably why there are so few humans around these days who can block a demon mind attack. They've all died out."

Tabi poured a generous glass of Pinot Grigio into a long-stemmed wine glass. "Enhanced human females are distantly related to the witches, right?"

"That's the general consensus, but nobody really knows," Raine said. "They could be their own species."

In that case, why couldn't there be enhanced males, since witches were both male and female? Oh, vampires and their natural enemy, the Kurjans, were male only, and Tabi only knew of the enhanced females they'd mated. "Have you ever heard of a vampire mating an enhanced human *male*?"

"A long time ago, but I'm pretty sure the Kurjans took out all enhanced human males before this new campaign they're now waging to end all enhanced females. Why do you ask?" The sound of pouring water came over the line. "Where's my bourbon, damn it?"

Tabi swirled her wine in the glass, watching the liquid catch the light. "I just didn't learn any of this from my guardian."

"Uh-uh," Raine said.

So he didn't believe her. It wasn't like he was focused on her, so that was all right. "Why are you still here, Raine?" He'd shown up at the anger management class, obviously to keep an eye on a former member, who had left quickly. A member who'd been a vampire-demon hybrid, much like Raine, although Raine was much more vampire than demon. "You should've left after Ivar did."

"My job isn't done," Raine said, his voice losing the congenial tone.

"What's your job?" She had to ask, even though it was obvious he wouldn't tell her.

He took a big drink, apparently having found his bourbon. "None of your business, demonness. Don't think of getting in my way."

She wouldn't. "Don't get all assholish with me. It's not necessary."

"My apologies." He didn't sound sorry.

"Who's in your bed, anyway?" she snapped, not really caring.

He took another drink. "Nobody. Just a nice lady I picked up at the grocery store in the fruit aisle."

An unwilling smile tilted Tabi's lips. "Fruit aisle? I'll have to try that." It had been way too long since she'd had a date. Her mind wandered instantly to the tall and sexy cop who wanted, for some reason, to save her. She sighed.

Raine cleared his throat. "I'm heading back to my nice fruit lady, considering she's had an hour of sleep to rest up for round number four. If you've found a human male who can stop a demon mind attack, I'd keep that information to yourself. Otherwise, he'll have a bullseye on his back. It wouldn't be nice to do that to the kind cop who's trying to help you."

She gasped. "How did you know?"

"I'm not a moron." Raine clicked off the phone.

She swallowed. Her questions had led to an obvious answer. She took her wine glass and went to her living room, peering out at the cop car parked by her curb with Evan O'Connell keeping watch over her.

What was she going to do with him?

* * * *

The engine quiet after an hour of being parked, Evan settled back in his Jeep, a cup of coffee next to him and an empty bag of chips on the passenger seat. He'd lost his appetite about a year ago and figured that eating junk food wasn't going to kill him, considering he was already dying.

His cellphone buzzed, and he answered the call with a swipe of his finger.

"O'Connell?" came through, a little scratchy.

"Hey, Mabel," he said, turning up the sound. "Did you get a hit?"

The eighty-year-old sighed loudly over the line. "Nope. Nothing on a Tabitha Rusko, Richard Goncharov, or anybody named Popov. Sorry, buddy."

"No worries. I didn't figure to get anything. Why are you working so late? This could've waited until morning," he said.

"Oh, I'll sleep when I'm dead," she cackled. "Besides, I'd rather get my hours in when the dumbass sheriff isn't here."

Evan snorted. "That kind of talk will get you fired, my friend."

"I notice you didn't disagree," she chortled.

No. There was no disagreement. The sheriff was buddies with the mayor and was also related by marriage. It was one of the things Evan had hoped to change before he moved on, but time was getting too short. He looked down at his shaking left hand. The attacks were getting worse. "Regardless, make sure somebody walks you out to your car tonight," Evan said.

"I will, if you promise to run for sheriff next fall," she returned, ending the call before he could answer.

Yeah, he wasn't going to be around in the fall. It was probably time to turn in his notice, but he wanted to wait until Tabi and his other friend, Abby, finished their anger management course and then got out of town. He might not be able to do much these days, but he could at least make sure both women were safe before quitting his job.

His head pounded, and he leaned back. The pain was becoming an odd reassurance to him that he was still alive. How weird was that?

A knock sounded on his window, and he jumped, reaching for his gun. "What in the world?" Anger replaced weakness, and he shoved open his door, standing and looming over the tiny blonde. "Never sneak up on an armed man," he said, his teeth clenched.

Tabitha huffed out a breath. "It isn't my fault you're sleeping in your car. Speaking of which, why are you camped outside my house?" In the dim moonlight, her eyes glowed like the deepest coal, and in her dark leggings and loose-fitting top, she looked young and cute.

Cute slayed him. Always had. "I was making sure that wacko from earlier didn't bother you," he admitted.

She sighed, ducking her head to stare at her bare feet. "You can't save everyone, Evan," she whispered.

It was the first time she'd used his given name. Apparently sitting outside her home at night and trying to protect her had granted him some sort of a closeness. "I'm not trying to save everyone." The itch between his shoulder blades wouldn't abate. How had the interloper known of Evan's illness earlier? Was it becoming that obvious? "I can still help you, Rusko."

She looked up then, way up, her expression one that caused intrigue. "What makes you think I need help?"

It was a good question. "It's my job," he answered, knowing it was a cop out.

She smiled. "Have you always had this desperate need to protect and defend?"

Ah. The motto on his police vehicle. He did love that Jeep. "I guess so." He scouted the quiet street and then gestured toward her bungalow. "You're safe tonight. Go on in and get some sleep." Her scent of mystery and unidentifiable flowers was going to drive him crazy, so he used his best official voice. The one most younger police officers jumped to obey.

The woman didn't so much as twitch. "I can't talk you into leaving?"

"No." It wasn't like he slept much these days, anyway.

"Then why don't you come inside, have some apple pie, and sleep on my sofa?" She clasped her hands together, looking like an innocent angel from times gone by.

Oh, he knew he had a thing for petite and fragile looking women, but this one had a strength to her that just plain and simply intrigued him. He needed to figure her out. But staying inside her house was a huge mistake, and he wouldn't make it. His radio buzzed before he could answer her.

"Evan? We have a nine-sixteen at 2827 East Beverly Street," Mabel said. "Again."

Damn it. He reached for the radio. "I'm en route." Then he nodded to Tabi. "Go inside and lock your doors. I have to go."

She lifted an eyebrow. "What's a nine-sixteen?"

He slid back into his seat. "It's a domestic violence call." He'd already been to the Baker house twice that month. Why the young bride wouldn't leave her husband, he didn't know. Maybe this time he could talk some sense into her.

Tabi frowned. "You're a detective. Shouldn't that call have gone to an officer?"

He nodded. "Yeah, but our two officers would've been called off by the sheriff. I won't be."

"Do you need help?"

He jolted. "No." Like the petite blonde could help him. "Just keep yourself safe tonight. I'll do a drive by later, but here's my cell number if you need help." He tugged a card out of his unused ashtray. "I mean it, Tabi. If you need help, call me."

She took the card, her expression bemused. "All right. Be careful." Then she turned and jogged back inside her house.

He sighed and started the engine, driving down the street.

"You know, you got a real hero complex, O'Connell," Mabel crackled through the radio. "What's the deal there?"

He rolled his eyes. "I'm just doing my job."

"Uh huh," she said. "Be careful at the Bakers' house. That moron is probably drunk again."

"Good," Evan said grimly. "Then I can arrest him this time."

Although, considering the idiot was the sheriff's youngest son, the asshole wouldn't stay in jail long. "We've got to clean up this town, Mabel."

"Wouldn't that be nice?" she cackled, signing off.

Yeah. He'd think of something.

Chapter 3

Evan's eyes were scratchy and his left leg weak when he strode into the room used for the anger management class. After arresting Baker the night before, he'd parked down the street from Tabi's house to keep watch, and once daylight had arrived, he'd spent a shitty day at the office, avoiding the sheriff since he'd arrested the asshole's kid the night before.

The smell of coffee wafted his way, and he turned to make an instant beeline for the table set up beneath the wide window, considering he'd missed dinner.

Dr. Lopez looked up from sitting on a metal chair at the edge of a circle of vacant metal chairs. "Hi, Detective. We have donuts and fresh cookies this fine evening." The shrink had dressed in dark jeans and a silky-looking pink shirt with her dark hair in a bob around her pretty face. Her forehead wrinkled. "It's so nice, but I can't figure out why the leader of the gambling anonymous meetings keeps bringing us food. He only stole our room once."

Evan shrugged and reached for a peanut butter cookie. "Maybe he feels guilty. Who knows?" The guy had done a complete turnaround, and if Evan didn't know better, he'd think one of Lopez's group members had had a little discussion with him. But nothing had been reported, and he had enough to worry about.

She smiled, her brown eyes sparkling. "I've gotten used to you attending the meetings. Isn't it time you sat and actually participated?"

He paused with the treat halfway to his mouth. "I'm not here as a participant."

She tapped her tennis shoe on the old wooden floor. "You might as well be, don't you think? I can tell that something is bothering you besides wanting to help Abby Miller, which I believe you already have. Why don't you participate?"

"Thanks, but no." If he was angry, it was because he was dying, and he didn't really need to share that fact with anybody. Abby Miller had been falsely accused of battery by her dirtbag ex, and the best deal Evan could get for her was probation so long as she attended these meetings. Of course, the ex was now dead. Thank goodness Abby had an airtight alibi for the murder.

As if reading his mind, Lopez frowned. "Are you here now because Abby's ex-husband was murdered?"

Evan shoved the cookie in his mouth and finished it before answering. "Don't you think it's odd that your group provided an alibi for each other?" The second they'd been questioned, the group claimed they'd all been having a pizza party when the murder had occurred. Abby should've been the prime suspect.

"No. They were all together. It's common for people in a group to try and make friends. I find it odd that you'd think that odd, considering they all just met a month ago. Why would any of them lie for near strangers?" She tilted her head.

"Good point," Evan admitted. Even so, something was weird with this group. With most of the members of the group.

Tabi swept inside, this evening wearing white slacks, a green blouse, and high heels with red bottoms. She whipped off what had to be designer sunglasses. "How did the domestic violence call go last night?"

"Fine." Evan's ribs still hurt from the bat, but he'd taken Baker down hard afterward, and that had felt good.

"Good." She poured herself a cup of coffee and strode over to sit by the shrink. "Good evening. How's the brain business, Mariana?" She sipped delicately.

The shrink smiled. "That's a tough question. If I say it's good, then people have problems. If I say bad, then I don't have patients, and I can't buy shoes like you're wearing. Those are stunning."

Tabi kicked out her leg and twirled her ankle. "Thanks. They give me four extra inches in height."

It was amazing she could be so graceful in the deadly things. Movement sounded near the door. Evan turned from staring at the sexy shoes to see Abby and her new friend, Noah Siosal, walk inside the room, holding hands. He wasn't one to judge, but meeting a guy in an anger management program probably wasn't the best move for Abby to make. Abby's ex had been an ass, and this guy was at least six-six and built hard. One punch, and he could kill a woman, without question. Plus, a sense of danger rolled off him.

She smiled at Evan, looking happy, her greenish-brown eyes sparkling.

Ah, damn it. Evan cut a harsh look at Noah, promising retribution if he hurt the brunette. Noah winked at him, his eyes as black as Tabi's but his hair a darker blond. In fact, they looked oddly alike, but Evan's background check on them hadn't pinpointed any relationship or past association at all.

Evan straightened. Besides a recent bar fight that had put Siosal into the group, he was clean. Yet something wasn't right.

The next person loping into the room set Evan's teeth even more on edge. Raine Maxwell, another muscled male that seemed out of place in the innocuous old school room. He had sharp green eyes, black hair, and a hoarse voice that was almost a low growl.

Evan knew a predator when he saw one. In fact, he'd once been one. A long time ago in the service.

Raine took a seat next to Tabi.

Fire lanced down Evan's spine. Why he felt so much for the blonde was a mystery he'd never have enough time to solve. Man, he really was losing it.

Then Johnny Baker walked in with his father, the sheriff, right behind him.

Evan went cold and then full hot. "I put you in a cell."

Johnny smiled and walked toward the circle. "Not for long." The punk was twenty years old with thick brown hair and beady brown eyes. He had his father's stocky build, but unlike the sheriff, he was muscled and his gut hadn't started to go to fat. Yet. His main hobby seemed to be beating up his bride.

The sheriff reached Evan's side. "We had an emergency hearing with the judge right after dinner, and Johnny was ordered to complete this anger management course, so the prosecutor agreed to drop all charges."

Evan's ears burned. "The judge, his uncle?" The sheriff's sister had married the local judge decades ago.

Sheriff Baker's jaw firmed. "There wasn't anything underhanded. This was a first offense, and it was probably a mistake."

Even though the entire room was watching, Evan leaned down into the face of his boss, fury deepening his voice. "This was a first offense because once again, the female victim refused to make a report. But this time, your son hit a cop with a fucking bat. Me. That matters."

Hatred glowed in the sheriff's dull eyes for a moment before being banked. "I'd watch it, O'Connell. You might be a buddy of the governor, which got you this job, but you work for me."

Johnny sat next to Dr. Lopez and smiled, his eyes hard. "I can't have anything like that on my record if I want to be a police officer."

Evan straightened. "Excuse me?"

Johnny lowered his chin. "I take the police officer entry-level civil service exam in two weeks. Good thing there's an opening in the department, right? I hope I have a chance of making it." His chuckle held a shitload of derision.

All the moron needed was a high school degree, and he had that. "You have to pass a drug test and a psych evaluation," Evan shot back. Although the sheriff would make sure he passed those, probably.

Raine Maxwell cleared his throat. "It appears as if we have a problem."

The sheriff turned on him. "Mind your own business."

Tabi cleared her throat. "Well, hello, Johnny. How are your balls? I believe I kicked them nearly through the top of your head when you and your buddies tried to accost me."

It was the attack that had been caught on tape. Evan should give her that video. Definitely.

Johnny swirled to look at her, and he did pale the slightest amount. "Oh, you and I aren't done."

Evan stepped forward. "Watch it, kid."

The sheriff grabbed his arm. "Detective O'Connell? You're not needed here, and I suggest you get back to work. Don't you have a murder to solve?" He turned and stared at Abby Miller. "I believe the, ah, grieving widow is right over there." The condescension in his tone had Abby's head jerking up and Noah's eyes narrowing.

Dr. Lopez read the room accurately. "Actually, I've requested that the detective join the group, since we have some tension here. Surely you're okay with that, Sheriff?" If that was the tone she used with her underage clients, she no doubt got definite results.

The sheriff paused and then smiled, his gaze running over the woman's form. "Of course. Anything for you, Dr. Lopez."

A low rumble sounded from Raine, barely audible.

Interesting. Evan pulled free from the sheriff before he could knock the guy out with one punch and lose his job. "Well, then. I guess I'll take a seat." He purposefully strode right over to sit next to Johnny. "You and I aren't done, either," he said, turning to face the shithead.

Tabi leaned back in her chair, watching him closely. "You're kind of fun when you're pissed off," she murmured, her dark eyes dancing.

"That's where you'd be wrong, darlin'," he returned, keeping everyone in the room in his sights. Threats were in every direction, and the feeling of missing something important wouldn't leave him.

Her small grin was nearly catlike and had the perverse result of turning him on. What was it with that woman?

The sheriff strutted toward the doorway. "O'Connell? Meet me at the station first thing tomorrow morning. I'd like an update on the case, and I have no doubt you'll be able to break the false alibi of the widow." He disappeared down the old hallway.

Abby sighed. "Detective? I'm so sorry to have gotten you into this mess. I did not kill my ex-husband." She'd been married to a lawyer, who'd been buddies with the sheriff and the judge, and there was no doubt she'd been railroaded in an arrest and then near conviction from a fake battery charge. Evan had used all his power to keep her out of jail and get her into probation and the anger management group before the ex had been murdered. "My alibi is solid."

Yeah. Her alibi was everyone in the room, except the shrink and Johnny. Something about a pizza party at Raine Maxwell's house, which just didn't set right. But it didn't make sense that these people, all from different walks of life, had conspired to kill a moron lawyer in a small Indiana town. "I hope so," Evan said, sitting back. "I do need to interview each of you soon, just so you know. We need follow-up information." Actually, he needed to compare their initial interviews with the second ones, just to see who was lying.

Although Monte Lofton had been an asshole, he'd been murdered, and Evan couldn't allow vigilante justice in his town.

Abby smiled. "I'll gladly be interviewed again, Detective. Switching topics, why don't you run for county sheriff in the fall? You'd basically just deal with this city and the few outlining areas, and you'd do a much better job than that jackass."

"Hey," Johnny protested. "That's my dad."

Abby turned on him. "No kidding. The judge is your uncle, too. It's time this baloney stopped in this town."

Evan would love to run for sheriff. His right ankle started to tremble, heading up to his knee. He pressed a hand on his thigh to try and stop the movement while ignoring the pain. "I'm afraid that's not in the cards for me," he said, effectively cutting off all debate with a harsh tone.

Dr. Lopez jumped and then reached for manila files from the briefcase by her chair. "Johnny? Since you're new to the group, let's start with you today. You were arrested for battery of your wife and a police officer."

Johnny rolled his eyes. "I didn't hit Louise, and the cop came at me first." He looked at Lopez's breasts. "I wasn't angry, either."

"My eyes are up here, junior," Lopez said, her tone hard.

Johnny grinned and looked up at her face. "Your eyes aren't your best feature."

Faster than Evan would've thought possible, Raine Maxwell had the kid out of his seat and slammed against the wall, only knocking over one chair in the movement.

Evan reached them instantly, shoving Raine off the kid.

Raine stepped back, his face cold. "One more word like that, and you won't need anger management. You won't need anything," he said, his voice a bizarre growl.

Dr. Lopez clapped her hands, her voice rising. "I can see we have a lot to discuss. Everyone take your seats. Now."

Evan studied the furious man, his instincts humming. "Apparently I'm not the only one protective of the women here," he murmured as Raine turned his attention on him. "I think I'll interview you first about Monte Loften's murder, Mr. Maxwell." There was absolutely no doubt in Evan's mind that Raine could kill. He probably had.

Raine smiled. "Looking forward to it, Detective."

Chapter 4

"If you need an alibi taking that twerp out, just let me know," Tabi whispered to Raine as she strode out of the abandoned schoolhouse after the useless anger management class. Johnny Baker was a waste of space, as far as she was concerned.

"Thanks," Raine said, not smiling, the darkness surrounding him. The early spring breeze rustled through the night, chilly and unwelcoming. At least it wasn't raining.

She nodded and moved down the crumbling cement sidewalk toward her car as Raine turned and jogged across the street to his silver truck. Stopping at her car, she paused, not surprised to see the detective heading her way through the night. "You really have a hard-on for me, don't you?" she murmured.

"Yes." Both of his eyebrows rose. "You sure have a way with words."

She unlocked her vehicle, her body flaring to life at his honest response. "I was raised by a woman who called it like she saw it." Sometimes the pain at losing Janet still took Tabi by surprise. Why did humans have to die? "Unless you're going to give up my video, I suggest you head to work like your boss ordered you to do."

Evan opened her door, his sexy scent of smoked honey wafting around. "I'll give you the recording."

She jolted and turned to face him directly. "What did you say?"

His blue eyes seemed darker than usual, deep with what looked like pain. "I'll give you the recording. Come down to the station tomorrow morning for one more interview, and then I'll take you to the bank myself."

It was as if he knew she was going to blow town the second she got her hands on the video, even though her business was here. She bit her lip. If she got the footage, she could meet Abby at the factory and give her instructions before running. Man, she hated to run.

Evan smiled. "You're sure thinking hard. Why don't you tell me what's really going on? I can protect you."

Warmth flushed her. The man truly believed that. The only way he could come close would be if she—no. No way. She shouldn't even think of that. Was it even possible? Did she want a mate?

"Tabitha? What's barreling through your head?" As if unable to help himself, he reached out and smoothed a lock of hair away from her face.

Shocking electricity zapped beneath her skin.

His brows drew down. "Did you feel that?"

She nodded. "Why are you now willing to give me the recording?"

He sighed and looked across the vacant street. "I don't like that the sheriff's kid is in the anger-management group with you, considering you definitely injured his pride along with his body. Chances are, he'll come after you. Since you're planning to run, I thought to make it easy for you." His gaze scouted the area, something he seemed to do often.

"Do you miss the service?" she asked softly, wanting to know more about him. Abby had told her that he'd served in the navy a while back.

He blinked. "Yeah."

"Why did you leave?"

His gaze shuttered closed faster than a bank vault.

"I know you're ill," she said quietly.

He gripped his left hand with his right. "I hoped nobody had noticed the tremors." Retreating instantly, he backed away. "Go home. I'll follow to make sure that kid doesn't mess with you tonight, and I'll pick you up in the morning to take you to the station. After your interview, I'll give you the video."

Without waiting for an answer, he turned and strode down the sidewalk toward his Jeep.

Her face still tingled from his touch. Bemused, she slipped into her BMW and ignited the engine, driving down the quiet street. She'd been hidden most of her life, and it wasn't like she had any close friends. After a quick mental debate, she dialed Abby's number.

"Hi, Tabitha. Are we getting to work tomorrow?" Abby immediately answered, sounding happy. Very happy.

"Yes," Tabi said. "Let's meet at noon at the factory, okay?" She'd hired Abby as her assistant when the woman had needed a job, and Abby's organizational skills had turned out to be phenomenal.

Abby chuckled. "A job that starts at noon. I love working for you."

Tabi turned a corner, keeping track of Evan's headlights behind her. "Can I ask you a question? It's kind of personal."

"Sure," Abby said, her voice light. She'd once been an enhanced human, and her mating with Noah was still fresh. "Ask me anything."

All right. Tabi took the next corner a little fast and forced herself to slow down, since a police officer was tailing her. Evan would probably give her a ticket. "When you mated Noah, or when he mated you, did you change a lot? I mean, did your personality change? Are you even done changing yet?" There was so much she didn't know about matings, considering she'd been raised by a human.

Abby was quiet for a minute. "I'm not sure if I'm done changing, and I haven't tried to heal myself of an injury yet. Other than that, I don't think I've changed personalities or anything. Shouldn't you know all of this stuff?"

Tabi winced. "I should, but I don't."

"Aren't you like a couple hundred years old?" Abby whispered.

Tabi jerked upright, her foot pressing harder on the gas pedal. "No," she snapped, oddly affronted. "Do I look centuries old?"

Abby coughed. She'd better not be laughing. "No. You look like you're in your mid-twenties, but I wouldn't think my mate was more than thirty or so, and he's four hundred years old. I just assumed. How old are you? In years?"

Tabi rolled her eyes. "I'm twenty-five. In years." Geez. Like she didn't know what Abby meant.

"Seriously?" Noah's voice came clearly over the line. "You're really only twenty-five?"

"Yes, vampire," Tabi snapped. "Or demon. Or hybrid. That's my real age." For goodness' sakes.

Noah cleared his throat. "Shit, Tabi. Don't you have family?"

"No," she said, trying not to hurt at saying the word. "I don't have anybody, Noah. I was raised by a human who I loved, and humans die." Like Evan O'Connell. He was going to die and probably soon.

A sleek luxury car swerved out of a driveway blanketed by trees, skidding in front of her.

"I have to go." She clicked off, prepared to ram the vehicle and beat the crap out of Johnny Baker. Until she saw the light hair of the driver. Holy crap. It was Richard Goncharov. So much for giving her three more days. She almost slowed down, until she caught Evan's headlights.

Panic seized her lungs. She had to get him out of danger. Taking a deep breath and forcing those lungs to work, she slammed her foot on the accelerator and swerved around Richard's town car.

* * * *

Evan flipped on his siren and punched the gas as the black car did the same, both of them chasing the white BMW. He drew abreast of the black car, seeing that Richard asshole driving. He lifted his flashlight and made a motion for the man to pull over.

The guy smiled, tightened his hold on his steering wheel, and shot forward into the darkened night.

Damn it. Evan set the flashlight on the seat, his adrenaline flowing and his temper blowing. He lowered his head and sped up, a primitive power filling him as he gave chase. Protocol dictated he call for backup, but for once, he let his instincts rule. He'd figure out why later.

The tail lights of the BMW flashed as Tabi took a corner fast, whizzing around a set of trees and heading toward the more industrial part of town. Smart. There would be fewer people in that area, and she could get out of the way and let him handle this jerk.

He reached for his phone and pressed her number, having taken it off her the night he'd arrested her.

"I'm kinda busy right now, Evan," she said, her voice gritty and determined.

So much for reassuring her. He grinned. "Listen to me, darlin'. Drive two miles and take a fast right into the Mills Pond Industrial Park."

"I don't need help here," she muttered, whipping around another corner like a Formula One driver.

Nice. The woman could drive. "Go to the farthest building—the one with the red metal roof. Then swing around it, and I'll take out this guy. Meet me at the station." He'd plow the luxury car right into the metal fence, once Tabitha had gotten safely out of the way.

"Um, this is weird for you, I'm sure. But I can handle my own problems." She slowed down and then zipped across a set of railroad tracks. "How about you go to the station?"

Was she joking? At a time like this? "Knock it off, Tabitha," he ordered. "Do what I said."

She drove right by the entrance to the Mills Pond Park, heading deeper into the darkness. "I've got this."

What the hell? She had this? "I mean it, Tabi," he snapped, driving faster toward Richard's car. If Evan couldn't get her cooperation, he'd have to come up with Plan B. "Turn into the next industrial complex."

"No." She drove right past it, with Richard right on her ass.

That was it. Evan punched the gas, swerved, and clipped the back of Richard's car. They both spun away from each other, correcting, and getting right back on track.

"Damn it, Evan," Tabi yelled, slowing down. "You don't understand any of this. Get out of here. Please." She flipped around and stopped.

Richard's tail lights flared as he skidded to a stop, facing the lights of the white BMW.

Evan slowed down. What the heck was going on? Some sort of weird game of chicken? Not on his watch. He slammed his foot on the pedal and lurched forward just as Richard did the same, both of them headed toward the BMW. Tightening his hold on the wheel, Evan jerked again, this time aiming for the left front of Richard's car. He spun them both into the metal fencing of another industrial complex.

His airbag exploded into his face, and he shook his head, jumping out of the vehicle while grabbing for his weapon.

The white BMW skidded to a halt next to him, and Tabi was out and running for him. "Evan!"

He grabbed her arm and pushed her behind him, trying to see through the steam hissing from the front of his Jeep. "Stay down." Then he crept to the side, his gun at ready, pointed at the innocuous black car. "Put your hands outside the vehicle. Now!" he yelled.

Nothing.

He crept closer, looking for movement.

Tabi came up on his side. "He's gone."

Evan's ears rang, and he shook his head, leaning down to confirm that the car was vacant. He levered up, looking around the area. "Where did he go?" There wasn't even any sound.

"Heck if I know." She sighed, sounding more put out than frightened.

Evan turned to face her. "What the hell is going on?" He'd just wrecked an official vehicle, and he hadn't even called it in.

Tabi looked him over, her eye gleaming through the darkness. "Are you all right?"

No. His brain was fried. None of this made a lick of sense, and that included his own actions. "Tabi—" he started.

She ran for him, jumping and wrapping her arms and legs around him. "You tried to save me." Then her mouth was on his. Soft and sweet, her tongue slipping inside his mouth with the taste of strawberries.

He clamped his hands on her tight ass and took over the kiss, going deep with no thought. For the briefest of moments, there were no thoughts, no fears, no pain. He forced himself to reclaim reality and leaned back, when all he wanted to do was bend her over the car and take what she was offering. "I have to call this in," he said, his voice gruff.

She smiled and leaned in to nip his bottom lip. "You'll never find him, and who the heck cares? Don't you want to take whatever pleasure you can right now? Just one night? You and me?"

His left leg began to tremble, and he shifted his weight to keep her aloft. A year ago, he would've said no. Even a month ago would've been a different situation. Fuck it. If he was going to die, he was going to have this night. "My place or yours?"

The trill of sirens jerked him out of the fantasy he was already living. Lights came into view—red and blue and swirling. He let her slide to the ground.

She put her hands on her hips. "Somebody must've seen us speeding."

"Right," he said, turning and rubbing the back of his neck. Yeah, he was going to get fired for this. No question about it.

"You didn't have time to get to your radio. It all happened so fast," she said, facing the oncoming lights.

He glanced down at her calm face. Just who the hell was Tabitha Rusko?

Chapter 5

Tabi stormed out of the police station after giving her statement for the third time to a detective who didn't seem to understand English. Either he would arrest her or not, and she'd made enough of a threat about her lawyers that she'd probably bought herself some time. It was a good bluff, anyway. She could find lawyers if she needed them. Either way, she was clear that the car chase and wreck had been the blond stranger's fault and not Detective O'Connell's.

Hence her shock when she ran into him right outside the brick building, and he was holding a box of his possessions. "Oh, they did *not* fire you," she exploded.

Evan turned toward her, his eyes dark. "Yeah, the sheriff has been looking for a way to get rid of me for a while." He jerked his head toward her BMW in the lot. "Why don't you give me a ride home, and you can tell me what's going on and exactly who this Richard is."

Heat nearly blew steam out of her ears. "Why are you taking this so calmly? Get in there and fight, Evan." She could see he was a fighter—especially with the bruises now down his neck from the wreck.

He turned to walk to her car and waited for her to unlock it before shoving his box in the back seat and settling into the front.

She slipped into the driver's seat and turned toward him. "Evan?"

He rested his head back. "I would fight it, but there's no use. I'd have to quit soon, anyway."

She reached out and put her hand over his. That electricity from the one kiss arched between them and she marveled at the feeling. Was it because he might be enhanced? Or maybe something was happening to her. Who knew. "Why?"

He opened his eyes, and the blue was fathomless. "I have Huntington's Disease. The tremors and limb weakness started about six months ago, and if I'm anything like my dad, I'll go downhill fast." His lower lip lifted in a wry smile. "I'd hoped to last long enough to get you and Abby out of probation and town, but it looks like I'll have to do so without my badge."

Man, she wanted to cold-cock that sheriff. "I've never met anybody like you," she admitted.

He grinned full-on this time, looking almost boyish. "A washed-up cop in a small town? We're a dime a dozen, beautiful." Now he sounded rueful.

She shook her head. "No. You try to save everybody, and you want to do the right thing. I bet you were a good soldier."

He sighed. "I did my job, and it wasn't pretty. I miss the teams, though. Got sick and had to leave."

The teams? He'd been a Navy SEAL? Figured. "So you got this job?"

He nodded. "I served with the governor way back when, and he did me a solid. I like it here. It would've been a good place to settle down and raise kids." He turned and pinned her with a look. "Now start driving and tell me what kind of trouble you're in. I can fix it before..."

Before he died.

She started the car, her mind spinning. A lot of immortals mated for political reasons. She'd never thought much about mating or love or forever before. What she did know was that Evan O'Connell was a good man who belonged on this planet a lot more than many immortals did. "I can save you," she whispered, turning and driving away from the station.

"Take the next left, and go for a while until Shavers Avenue turns into Fourth Street," he said quietly. "Nobody can save me, sweetheart."

She followed his directions, her hands shaking lightly on the wheel. Was she crazy to even think about this? "If you could live, possibly forever, what would you do?"

He rolled his neck. "Forever? I don't know. First, I'd run for sheriff and turn this county around. Clean out the bastards screwing everything up. Then I'd settle down and have some kids. Then, who knows. Forever is a long time, and there's probably a lot to do." He chuckled. "What about you?"

She'd never really thought about helping other people. "I'd, ah, try to survive, I guess. And I'd start a lucrative business." Which she'd already done, if she could just get the prototypes finished. Safety came from money, and she knew it. "You're a better person than I am." Than anybody she'd ever met.

He chuckled. "Honey, I'm not even close. I did things in the military that keep me up at night, but I'd do them again if I had to. You're meeting me at the end of my life and end of my illness. At full strength, I would've probably already beat the crap out of the sheriff and his son. The judge, too." He sighed. "I would've liked to have known you before all of this. Of course, you probably wouldn't have liked me. I wasn't so easygoing."

Right. Even now, he was being sweet. "Do you believe in, well, things you can't see?"

"Like germs?"

She coughed. "No. Like, I don't know, vampires?"

His chin dropped to his chest. "Oh, honey. I was afraid of that. The weird Richard guy who convinced you he could hurt your mind. Are you in some sort of cult?"

Cult? She sucked in air. "No. I'm not easy to manipulate." Wow. He had totally read her wrong. So he wasn't exactly open to a different reality. If she told him she was a demonness, he'd probably try to take her to the psych ward. Something told her there wasn't enough time for that. She tried a different tack. "If you had the chance to live forever, would you take it?" she asked.

"In a heartbeat," he said quietly, running his wide hands down his jeans. "So long as I kept my soul."

She swallowed, turning into the driveway of a small brick house set against a series of trees. "I hope you're sure about that." This was something she could do. If she mated him, then she was partially responsible for all the people he helped through eternity, right? That had to go in the plus column for her life. Heat flushed through her. Could she do this?

"It doesn't matter." He took her hand. "I think you should stay the night in my guest room, at least until we find that Richard who won't leave you alone. Once you give me the whole story, I'll call in some favors I'm owed, and we'll track him down. I promise."

She couldn't breathe. This was nuts.

He lifted her hand to his mouth. "Would you stay the night?"

She squared her shoulders, tingles wandering up her arm just from one kiss of his lips. Her palm flashed hot and painful against his touch. Holy immortal crackers. The mating mark pulsed on her palm—the one that appeared when a demon found their mate. Oh, there was something between them. That was for sure.

"I'm definitely staying," she whispered.

* * * *

Evan escorted Tabi into his small brick home, flipping on lights as they went. Having her in his space was making his clothes feel too constricting. Man, she was beautiful. There was something wild and untamed about her, especially after that car race, that made him shove his hands in his pockets to keep from reaching for her.

His dogs ran up, both panting. "This is Buck and Lewey." They were long-haired mutts, part black lab and part who knows what, and he adored them. "Outside, guys." They obediently ran for the back door, and he let them free. "Are you hungry?" He might have a waffle or two in the freezer.

"No." She looked at the freshly polished wooden floors and the hand-crafted fireplace mantle with self-placed river rock. "This place is lovely. Did you do all of this yourself?"

His ears heated. "Yeah. It's probably dumb, but I wanted to leave something complete behind. Something I'd created myself." Shaking himself out of it, he exited the living room and showed her down the wide hallway to the guest room, which held his grandmother's furniture that he'd refinished. He'd see her soon. Then he chuckled. He'd be okay after a good night's sleep and then could help Tabi out of this mess. Once he got her out of his space he could take some deep breaths. Alluring was too tame a word for her.

She stared at the cherrywood dresser. "What's Huntington Disease?"

He stilled. "Oh. It's a rare and progressive brain disorder that demolishes physical and mental abilities. Before you ask, it's genetic, and there is no cure. It's fatal, and my dad died from it." Sharing with her helped, somehow.

She tossed her purse onto the bed. "What about your mother?"

"Car wreck when I was nine. No other relatives." The blonde was a sweetheart in trying to connect. He didn't need connections, although she was a temptation, that was for sure. That mysterious and feminine scent of hers was heating his blood in a way that made him feel healthy again.

"What does your room look like?" She turned, those black eyes guileless.

"Oh." Of course, she wanted the tour, and he had redone the entire home. His chest puffed out just enough to make him feel like a moron. "I'll show you the rest of the house." If he got her anywhere near his bed, he might lose the control he was reaching for like a starving man.

She made appropriate noises at the rest of the house, until they reached his room. Then she gasped. "It's so...you."

He felt like shuffling his feet so he stood taller. "Thanks. I made the furniture in the garage, which I turned into a woodshop." The furnishings were oak with hand-carved designs of different angles of crests of his ancestors, who'd come over to the States from Scotland. He moved to flip off the light.

She stepped in front of him, looking up, a light pink flushing across the porcelain skin of her enticing face. "I want to stay in here tonight."

In another time, he would've already had her on the bed. But even he didn't need a pity fuck. "I appreciate it, sweetheart, but it's just not a good idea."

Her face cleared and her mouth opened slightly. "Oh. I see. You, um, can't?"

He coughed and then laughed full-on. When was the last time he'd felt humor? When he calmed, he tugged on a piece of her hair. "Yeah, I can. Parts of me still work just fine—at least for now." It was a sobering thought, and he didn't like it. "You've had an adrenaline-filled night, you must be scared of that wacko in the car, and I hit you with the fact that I'm dying. None of those are good reasons to make yourself vulnerable."

She tilted her head, studying him. "Do I look like I feel vulnerable to you?"

"No." She looked like temptation and innocent sin, which was a contradiction he'd never imagined. Until now.

She moved into him, sliding her hands from his abs up to his chest, humming in what sounded like appreciation. "Do I look scared or like I feel sorry for you?"

His cock pressed so hard against his zipper that he barely hid a wince. "I'm trying to do the right thing here."

She curled her fingers and her nails bit into his skin through his T-shirt. "So am I." With that illusive statement, she levered up on her toes and kissed him. Her lips were full and soft, and a temptation he'd never be able to deny, regardless of noble intentions.

He let her play for a moment and then slowly took control of the kiss, deepening it when she slid her hands beneath his shirt and across his abs. His stomach undulated, and he forced himself to slow down. While she was a siren, he was twice her size, and he had to be careful.

Her touch was hot. Very. He leaned back, desire clawing through him. "Are you sure?"

"Yes." She tugged on his shirt, and he ducked his head to let her yank it up and away.

Something caught his eye, and he grasped her right hand, turning it over to look at a tattoo on her palm. Winding vines surrounded the letter R, looking both ancient and delicate. It was beautiful work, whoever had drawn it. How had he not noticed it before? "R for Rusko?" he murmured.

"Yes."

"It looks fresh." Maybe he wasn't the only one trying to hold on to the past.

Her chuckle swam down his skin and landed in his balls. "You could say that. It's very new."

"It's stunning."

"I'm glad you think so," she said, her eyes nearly looking silver for the briefest of moments. Then she reached for the snap of his jeans.

Chapter 6

Tabitha saw the second Evan gave up the fight to protect her for her own good. His eyes shifted, and his shoulders went back. Smoothly, he lifted her and easily carried her to the bed. His strength gave her a slight pause. If he was this strong as a human, what would he be like immortal? Then he leaned over and kissed her, and she forgot all about reservations.

The cop could kiss.

He set her on her back, one knee next to her on the bed, his mouth working hers as if they had all the time in the world. His lips were firm, and he explored her, sliding his mouth away from hers and along her face, nipping where her jaw met her neck.

She shivered, her body lighting on fire.

Slowly, gently, he drew her blouse up along her ribcage with both hands, his fingertips caressing and teasing her rib cage. She reached for him, sliding her hands through his thick hair like she'd wanted to do for weeks. Then she tugged.

He paused, his palms warm against the sides of her breasts.

She smiled. "I don't need slow, and I'm not breakable."

His eyes burned the dark hue as dusk gave up the fight to night. "I'll go as slow as I want, and baby, I won't break you." Then he pulled her shirt over her head and looked down, male satisfaction curving his lips. "God, you're beautiful."

She wish she'd worn her fancy bra instead of the comfortable cotton one, so she reached for the front clasp and released it. "I'm okay," she murmured, having fun. She wasn't exactly well endowed, but by the flaring of his eyes, he didn't seem to mind.

He reached for her, palming both breasts, no longer holding back. Electricity zipped through her skin and right to her core, and she arched against him, surprised at the intensity. Then he leaned down and kissed her again, taking control in the smoothest of ways.

Everything felt so good. *He* felt so good against her. She dug her fingers into the still hard planes of his chest, sliding her palms down to dig into each rippling muscle in his abs, need rioting through her so fast she could barely breathe.

He released the button of her pants and slid them down her legs, standing by the bed as he did so. "We're leaving the shoes on, baby." Watching her, seeing more of her than she'd like, he shoved his jeans down, revealing what she'd suspected. The cop was built. Like very nicely built.

Need and want coursed through her, powerful in the demand. Vulnerability hinted inside her for a second.

He must've caught her look, because he slid both hands up her thighs and placed a kiss right above her belly button. "I won't hurt you, Tabi. I promise."

She couldn't fool him. He was too important, and so was this. "I want to mate you. We'd be tied forever," she whispered, not even sure what that meant. But at least he'd be alive.

He paused. "Mate?"

Oh, crap. The guy was too grounded in his own reality. "Yes. Please say yes."

Confusion clouded through the desire in his expression. "Honey, I don't have long, and mating doesn't exist. Not like you said it." He brushed her hair away from her face, his touch infinitely gentle. "I'm not sure what you're caught up in, but I can help you." He started to draw back.

"No." She yanked him down and pushed his shoulder so he'd roll on his back. Levering with her knee, she slid atop him, straddling all of his smooth and strong body, her heels on the bed. "Don't stop. Forget I said anything. I'm not in a cult, and you're not taking advantage of me." She told him all she could, and he'd said he would want to live forever. If this actually worked, and he was pissed, they'd have eternity to work it out. If they stayed together. Nobody said they had to stay together. Not really.

He reached up, cupping her face while his cock pulsed against her core, obviously straining to get in. The feeling was too much, and the ache inside her intensified. "You understand I can't make any sort of claim here, right? I'm temporary, Tabitha."

Claim? The guy sounded like a vampire for a minute. "What if you weren't dying?" she whispered, unable to keep her body from rubbing against him. Pleasure burst through her with a promise of more. A lot more.

"Then I'd be inside you right now, making you say my name." As if going on instinct, he slipped his head to the nape of her neck, twisting his fingers in her hair and taking control. He tugged her head to the side and then drew her down. "I'm done fighting us both. Tell me now if you want this."

Oh, she wanted him. Whether she wanted what she was about to do, she wasn't sure. "I want you. Inside me and now," she said, going for honesty.

"Good enough." He kissed her then, putting everything into it this time. Power, male, strength.

She moaned, her hands curling into his shoulders.

He rolled them again, blanketing her, broad and long. So much bigger than her. He reached down, one finger gently sliding inside her. "Oh, Tabi. You're ready, baby."

She gasped, throwing her head back. Yeah, she was wet and ready for him. Fast. Really fast. She scraped her nails down his flank, over his hip, and touched his length. Full and pulsing, hard and long, he was ready, too. She chuckled, the sound hoarse. "Right back at you."

He chuckled, the sound pained. Then he licked along her jaw and headed between her breasts.

She grabbed his hair and pulled him back on. "I'm all for playing and foreplay, but I want you. Now." Everything hurt—she ached way too much for him. "We can go slow and play later."

His nostrils flared. "Hold on." He reached into the bedside drawer, pulling out a condom.

It would take too much time and maybe get him to stop if she explained that he didn't need that, so she let him roll the useless thing on himself. He smiled and kissed her nose, pausing at her entrance and seeking her eyes, as if making sure one more time that she wanted this.

To prove it, she reached around and clenched his very fine buttock.

His nostrils flared, and he entered her, going slowly and allowing her body time to accept him.

The moment was intimate and the feeling delicious. Different than ever before in a way she couldn't quite grasp, and she shoved any indecision to the side. It was too late to worry about that.

He finally pushed all the way inside her, taking her.

Much too late.

* * * *

If Evan was going to die, this was a hell of a way to go. Tabi breathed out, her face flushed, her body warm beneath his. Those glorious black eyes looked silver again in the dim light, and her pretty pink lips pursed in an o. "Are you all right?" he rumbled, holding his weight off her with one elbow.

"Yes," she breathed, lifting her knees and giving him even more access to go deeper.

She was wet and tight around him, her internal walls gripping with a strength that made him want to start pounding inside her like a randy teenager. Instead, he pulled out and pushed back in, watching her carefully to make sure he didn't hurt her. She gasped and arched against him, her nails shredding the skin on his ass.

He did it again, holding on to control like always.

She did something inside her that gripped him even tighter, and he clenched his teeth. "Go, Evan. Now," she whispered, her voice the sexy hoarseness of a bombshell from days gone by.

Unable to stop himself, he plunged out of her and powered back in, setting up a strong rhythm that bounced her pretty breasts on her chest. Leaning down, he captured a nipple and lightly bit.

She cried out, wrapping her legs around his waist.

He leaned up. "I'm going to spend some serious time playing with those later tonight," he warned her, his body working on its own for that elusive release just out of his reach.

"Promises," she whispered, the cords in her neck straining as she met his thrusts with her own, stamping a claim on him he'd never felt before.

Right now, he was caught up in the moment and in the exquisite woman beneath him. Later he'd feel the remorse that they were so temporary and regret not meeting her earlier in his life. Right now, she was all heat, wildcat, and female. He slid his knees up and reached beneath her for the small of her back, lifting her up to meet his fierce pounding.

"Yes," she moaned, reaching almost desperately for his waist and digging in. "More. I need you. Here. More." She tried to pull him down.

Still powering inside her, he pushed his knees out and lay over her, overcome for the first time in his life. She was special, and there was no question about that. Possessiveness took him, shocking since it was impossible to keep her. He kissed her hard, his tongue diving inside her mouth.

She kissed him back, her hands frantic, her body tightening around him. Her right hand clamped on his hip, and her other manacled his hair, turning his head and kissing beneath his jaw.

Fire flashed along his hip, and a sharp pain ticked through his neck.

She cried out, arching against him, her body shaking so hard with her orgasm that his eyes nearly rolled back in his head. He kept up the pressure, sure to hit her clit, and let her ride out the waves.

With a soft sigh, she breathed out, licking his neck. Then, swear to God, she purred.

He lifted up, wanting to see her eyes. They looked all silver and only spurred him higher. He gripped her hip, pounding inside her, his entire being caught up in this moment.

She turned her head, revealing her smooth and vulnerable neck.

He pressed his lips to her jugular, electricity shooting down his spine so fast his entire back burned. His balls enlarged, and with absolutely no thought, he sank his teeth into her neck until he tasted blood. Then he exploded, his body shaking with an unreal force as an orgasm spiraled him nearly into darkness.

He stilled inside her, his dick still jerking with aftershocks. It took several moments, but he slowly came back into himself. There was blood on his lips. "Tabi. I bit you." He blinked, trying to concentrate. Then he leaned back to survey the damage to her delicate skin. Yep. He'd bitten her. He looked up to apologize, shocked.

Her sleepy grin stopped him short. "I bit you, too." Then she patted his chest. "You're very good in bed, Evan."

He couldn't find words, so he withdrew, almost smiling at her soft sound of protest. "Did I hurt you?" He'd never drawn blood with a woman before. Hell. He'd never bitten one, either.

"Nope. I'm good." She stretched like a satisfied cat. "But sleepy. Let's take a break."

A break? He wouldn't be able to go for a while. Instantly proving him wrong, he started to harden again. What was it about this woman?

"Hold on." He slipped off the bed and moved to the adjacent bathroom to dispose of the condom, strode into the living room to let the dogs in, and then returned to her.

The woman was already asleep.

He let himself look his fill. Her light hair splayed out in every direction like sunshine, a perfect backdrop for her pale skin and firm body. Her breasts were small, with light pink nipples that matched her lips. He tried not to wish for things that could never be. Even now, after a truly spectacular time with her, his body ached. His hip hurt like he'd been burned, and his head was starting to pound.

He lifted her easily off the bed and pulled back the covers, setting her inside as gently as possible. Then he slid in beside her, turning to spoon his body around her. For as long as he was able, he'd protect her. Then he'd come up with a plan for when he was gone, which was going to be soon.

It already felt like he had a fever.

Chapter 7

God, she was hot. Burning hot. Tabi opened her eyes, blinking several times as memories rushed in. "Evan?" she whispered, turning to where the heat emanated from.

He lay on his stomach with the covers pushed down to the dip of his waist. Sweat dotted his entire back, which was flushed a deep red. The muscles bunched and tightened as she watched.

"Evan?" she repeated, rolling to place her hand between his shoulder blades. "Ouch." She jerked back, her palm slightly burned. Awareness swept through her, and she sat up, poking his sweating shoulder. "You have a fever. A way too high fever." When he didn't move, she prodded harder. "Wake up, Evan."

His face was turned away from her, so she scrambled over him, standing by the side of the bed and leaning down. More sweat rolled down his ruddy face, and his hair was sopping wet. She smoothed strands away from his forehead. "Please wake up." Then she leaned down and shut her eyes to listen.

He was breathing, but it was labored.

Oh, this was so bad. Had she been too late to save him? Still naked, she ran to the guest room and yanked her phone from her purse, dialing quickly.

"What?" Raine growled into the phone. "It's too early to call, demon."

"Who are you calling a demon? That just isn't nice," a sleepy female voice muttered. A different voice than from the one the other day.

Tabi's legs trembled. "I need help, Raine. I might've goofed up. Or maybe it's the illness. I don't know." Her voice rose as panic tried to take her.

"Okay. Slow down. Where are you?" Covers rustled softly as the vampire obviously got out of bed.

She quickly rattled off the address. "Come as soon as you can." She ended the call and ran back into Evan's bedroom, stopping short as a wave of power hit her. Whoa. What was that? Her hands shook, but she quickly put on her clothes from the day before. "Evan?"

He still didn't move.

All right. That fever couldn't be good for him. She hurried into the master bathroom and doused several towels in cold water, returning to gently place them on his back and behind his neck. Then she winced as she saw the clear outline of her bite right beneath his jaw.

Her fangs were small but sharp. Very rarely used.

She quickly braided her hair out of her face while watching Evan, her stomach cramping. What if she'd just sped up his death? Oh, she should've done more research before trying to mate him. What the hell did she know about the process?

A loud knock sounded on the outside door. She jumped and then ran through the house to yank it open.

Raine Maxwell stood in the dawn light, his hair mussed and his jeans wrinkled. A dark tee stretched tight his wide chest. "Are you all right?"

She gulped and nodded, pulling him inside. "I'm fine. Although I may have really screwed up."

Raine stepped inside and looked around, his green eyes blazing. "Where are we? This isn't your place."

"It's Evan's," she said, her breathing shallow.

Raine's eyebrow rose. "You killed the cop?"

"I don't know." She grabbed the vampire's arm again and yanked him. "This way."

Raine sighed and followed her through the house and down the hallway. "I thought he was on your side. Why would you kill him?"

They reached the master bedroom, and Tabi pointed inside. "I mated him."

Raine jerked to a halt, and his eyes widened. "You fucking did what?"

Tabi winced. "I mated him. He's a nice guy, and he should live forever."

Raine shook his head like she'd thrown water up his nose. "You mated a *human* male?"

She gulped. "Yeah. I think so. I mean, I've never done it before, but

I bit him and I think I marked him." She held up her hand to show her family marking on her palm. When a demon found their mate, a marking appeared with the first letter of their surname, kind of like a family crest. The marking transferred during the mating.

"You think?" Raine snapped, stepping into the room. He stopped cold. "Wow. That's a bucket full of power coming from that bed."

The wooden floor was cold on her feet but solid. Very solid. "I know," she admitted.

Raine shook his head and continued forward, looking down at the burning-up male on the bed. With one finger, he slid the sheet down to reveal Evan's hip and the perfect branding of the Rusko marking. "Yep. You sure branded him."

Tabi's eyes widened as she studied the marking. It was far more delicate than the military tattoo on Evan's shoulder. "He bit me, too." Her neck still hurt, and she sent healing cells to the injury. "Does that usually happen when an immortal mates an enhanced human?"

"I don't think so," Raine said, tugging the sheet back into place. "But we don't know much about enhanced males, since there aren't supposed to be many, if any, still alive." He stepped away from the bed, leaned against the wall, and stared at the silent male still sweating profusely.

"What now?" Tabi asked, her legs weak again. What had she been thinking?

"Hell if I know," Raine admitted. "You're young to mate, and he's a human who was dying of some sort of disease that I could sense."

"Huntington's Disease," she confirmed. "But mating should cure him, right?" Although she wasn't as strong as she'd be one day, once she'd lived a century or two. Surely that couldn't hurt Evan. Or could it? Yeah, she should've done a lot more research, somehow, before she'd risked his life like this. She was so impulsive sometimes.

"Shit," Raine said. "You might've just created a monster. We really don't know much about enhanced males. There's even a theory that they're more related to dragon shifters than witches."

Tabi coughed. "There's no such thing as dragon shifters."

Raine crossed his arms. "Yeah, there is. I guess it's a big secret, but it's getting out these days. Secrets never stay for long, you know." He shook his head. "We need to find out more, just in case I have to put him down."

No way. Tabi shook her head. "You will not harm him."

"Might not have a choice," Raine said. "Either way, we have to make a call."

Tabi's eyes widened. "No. Please."

"Yeah. We're calling the queen." Raine reached for the phone in his pocket. "God help us."

* * * *

Evan burned from the inside out. So this was what dying felt like. It hurt.

He tried to open his eyes, but his eyelids stayed shut. Lights swirled behind his closed eyelids, white and bright, muted and colorful. Pain took him, head to toe, centering in his chest like a ball of fire. Memories assailed him. His childhood, his parents, even his football coach. He relived his time in the military, made friends, lost brothers, then got sick.

Finally, the night with Tabitha.

At the thought of the stunning woman, he growled.

"What the fuck was that?" a male voice snapped.

Everything inside Evan bunched and coiled. He opened his eyes and jumped out of the bed, looking for the interloper.

Raine Maxwell leaned against his bedroom wall, a phone in his hand, his eyes a piercing green.

The smell of woman caught Evan's attention, and he swung his gaze to Tabitha. *His.*

She stared at him, her eyes a wide black catching all the light in the room. "Evan?" she asked.

The rumble of her voice spurred the beast suddenly inside him, and he reached for her arm, jerking her behind him. She fell against the bed and sputtered, standing up. "What the heck?" she whispered.

Evan turned to face Raine, his chin going down. He clenched his fingers into fists and prepared to charge.

"You're naked," Raine said reasonably, slipping his phone into his front pocket. "I'm ready to go if you are, and it'd be a good fight, but you are buck-assed nude. If you want to grapple, that's fine, but I'd really appreciate it if you'd at least put on some jeans. Dude."

Evan looked down at his nude body. His very hot, sweaty, tingling body. The room began to spin around him, and he staggered. He growled. Really growled. What the holy hell was happening?

"You're okay." Tabi's voice cut through the cloud in his brain, and her soft touch on his arm eased the raging turmoil inside him. "Let's sit you on the bed before you fall down."

Evan looked toward the one threat in the room, appeased that Raine hadn't moved away from the wall.

"Here you go," Tabi said, her voice slightly higher than normal. Stress? Fear?

He reacted to her emotion and sat, pulling her onto his bare lap. The room smelled like sex...and sweat. She struggled against him, and he tightened his hold, forcing his gaze to focus again.

"Well," Raine drawled. "This is certainly interesting."

Evan swallowed, barely catching enough spit in his mouth to ease down his desert dry throat. "Why are you in my bedroom?"

Raine smiled, the sight not even close to being amused. "Tabitha? Want to field that curveball?"

She partially turned to face Evan, her butt nicely placed over his suddenly aching cock. "Well, now. I need you to keep an open mind."

Evan's gaze jerked from her face to Raine's.

The man chuckled and held up a hand. "No. Not that open. God."

Tabitha sighed and patted the side of Evan's face. "Concentrate, would you? It's like this. Well, I'm a demonness, and I mated you when we had sex."

Oh God. Evan deliberately, very gently, set her next to him and stood to face Raine. "You're a part of this cult?" What had he been thinking to sleep with her? His head pounded like he'd been punched repeatedly with a rock, but he'd deal with his illness later. Right now, he had to help the woman he apparently had just taken advantage of during the night. He'd known she was troubled. "Maxwell?"

Raine sighed. "Cult? What's he talking about?"

Tabi started to stand and then halted when Evan glowered at her. "It's a long story, but there's no cult. Honest, Evan. You're an enhanced male, maybe part dragon or witch or something, and I mated you." She frowned, peering closer. "Do you feel any better? Maybe stronger?"

Actually, he felt like his head was about to blow right off his neck from the pounding agony at his temples. "Okay. Here's what's going to happen." He needed to drink a glass of water to stop sounding like he'd been chewing soup cans all night. "Tabi? I'm going to take you to Dr. Lopez to get some help, while Mr. Maxwell and I go to the station. I think you're under arrest, Raine." He'd get the threat behind bars before making sure Tabi was cared for.

"You were fired," Tabi reminded him.

Raine's eyebrows rose. "Fired? What did you do?"

Oh yeah. Evan had forgotten. He eyed Raine. "Did you kill Monte Loften? As part of your cult or something? Is Siosal involved, and did he get Abby Miller to help?" It would make sense since they all had provided an alibi for each other. What had he gotten Abby and now Tabi involved in when he'd all but forced them into that anger management group? "Is the shrink part of the cult?"

Raine scratched his head. "Did the mating scramble his brain, do you think?"

"I don't know," Tabi said softly. "He has a pretty high fever. Maybe he's delirious."

"A fever?" Raine twisted his mouth, obviously thinking. "That's rare. I don't think Abby got a fever when Siosal mated her. I've never heard of that, but I guess it could be possible. We'll know soon enough."

Tabi stood, pausing when Evan instinctively turned to keep his body between the woman and Raine. "You did not text the queen," she whispered tersely.

"Queen?" Evan said, anger flushing through him hotter than his fever. "Your cult has a fucking queen?"

Raine rubbed the whiskers along his jawline. "Maybe you should show him the marking?"

Tabi gasped. "Maybe. Look at your hip, Evan."

Was this a trick? Evan looked at his left hip and then his right, seeing a perfect tattoo of the R that had been on Tabi's hand. It looked kind of small on his hip, set crooked and leading to his ass. He gingerly touched it, noting the slight pain. His eyebrows rose, and fury lanced his chest. Had they somehow knocked him out during the night? Had he been poisoned or drugged? He felt like it. "You *branded* me when I was asleep? With your fucking cult sign?"

Raine knocked his head back against the wall. "For God's sakes. He's too dumb to be immortal."

Tabi sighed and wrung her hands together. "You're just not getting this, Evan. Please pay attention this time."

He turned fully to face her, that weird growling sound emerging from his gut. The room wavered and then started to spin around him dizzily. They had drugged him.

It was his last thought before falling hard into unconsciousness.

Chapter 8

A pounding not inside his head jerked Evan awake again, and he bolted upright on his bed. His bedroom was empty. He lifted his head, smelling Tabi's alluring scent right before sensing threats. He shoved from the bed and yanked his jeans on, drawing his backup gun from his dresser and padding barefoot down the hallway toward the living room.

Raine and Tabi were at the door, and they let in a definite threat. The man had black hair, deep black eyes, and a wide chest. He was as tall as Raine and moved like he could fight. His expression was pissed off, without question. "Maxwell," he said, his slight brogue Scottish.

"Who the fuck are you?" Evan snapped, pointing the gun at the newcomer.

The guy looked his way. One very dark eyebrow rose. "He's got power."

Ah shit. Another cult member. Evan sidestepped into the room, keeping all three in his sights. "Tabitha? Behind me. Now."

She threw up her hands and strode toward him, letting him put his body nearer the men. "Evan. Listen to me."

"Against the wall. Both of you." Evan gestured with the gun, feeling in control for the first time that day, although his temples still thrummed. "What drug did you give me?"

The newcomer gave Raine a side-eye look. "You drugged him?"

"Of course not." Raine pulled the guy inside. "What the hell are you doing here, Adare?"

Adare kept his focus on Evan. "I was on my way to fetch my wayward mate when the king asked me to detour here and lock down a threat until he arrived."

Not another freaking cult member. "Do you guys have a size requirement, or what?" Evan muttered.

Raine paused and looked at Adare. "You're working with the Realm?"

"No, but I'm not working against them, and when the king asks for a favor, it seems prudent to grant it. For now." Adare's brogue deepened and he tilted his head to look at Tabi behind Evan. "Who's the demonness?"

Raine sighed. "Tabitha Rusko and Evan O'Connell, this is Adare O'Cearbhaill."

Adare jolted. "Rusko? I thought you'd all died out. Aren't you crazy?"

Tabi stamped her foot. "I am not crazy, and we did not die out. Well, I'm alive, anyway."

This was too bizarre. "Where are my dogs?" Evan asked.

"Outside," Tabi whispered.

Raine shrugged. "All righty then. I'm out of here." He began to move outside, into what looked like late afternoon.

Evan had slept all day? "Stop, Raine. I will shoot you," Evan growled.

"Listen, copper," Raine said, looking even more put out than he had earlier. "No offense, but the Maxwells like to stay off the Realm's radar, and they're about to descend on you like moss on a river rock."

Evan stiffened. "Are we in danger?"

Raine lifted a shoulder. "Probably."

Evan had to get Tabi out of there.

She pushed to his side. "You can't be leaving me with the Realm," she protested.

Raine smiled. "I sure can. Good luck, you two." He hustled away faster than Evan would've thought possible.

"Don't shoot him," Tabi said. "He didn't do anything wrong, except leaving me for the Realm, and I'll handle him later. Somehow."

The Realm must be the name of the cult. Evan focused on Adare. "You said something about your wayward mate." Was there a woman in danger from this guy? While Evan wasn't a cop any longer, he couldn't let this massive man harm a woman.

"Aye," Adare said, holding up his right palm to show a faint tattoo. "The brat has sat on my last nerve, and I've allowed her enough freedom." The tattoo was different from the one on Tabi's palm and now on Evan's ass. Why didn't they have the same tattoo? The Scottish guy looked Evan up and down. "How are you feeling?"

What the hell? "I told you to get against the wall." Evan aimed his weapon between Adare's eyes.

The guy actually rolled them. Seriously.

Tabi hovered next to Evan. "Have you ever seen an enhanced male human? Especially one who got mated?"

Adare slowly shook his head, watching Evan closely. "Nope. I thought the Kurjans killed them all—mainly because there was something off with the biology of enhanced human males."

Tabi audibly gulped. "Off? Like what?"

"Like when their chromosomal pairs grew to the immortal level, they became themselves times a hundred. Assholes became serious assholes, and so on." Adare smiled. "I hope this guy wasn't an asshole."

"He wasn't. I don't think," Tabi said.

"Enough with this cult bullshit," Evan barked. "I will shoot you."

Adare's eyebrows rose. "He seems like an asshole. I've also heard something about testosterone and strength in mated human males that's unreal and had other species wary, which is probably why they were killed off." Then he stiffened, lifting his head and glancing outside. "Well, now. I guess I didn't have time to do much here. Good. Truth be told, I'm not sure what should be done with you, human."

Oh, man. Did these people think they were aliens or something? Evan shook his head. "How big is your cult?" They kept coming out of the woodwork.

As if on cue, bodies poured inside through both the back and front doors, all huge and wearing black clothing outfitted with several weapons. Evan backed Tabi to the fireplace, his gun at the ready, keeping his body between her and any threat. As soon as the house was swept, the soldiers all exited, save one large bastard with messy brown hair and eyes hidden by dark sunglasses. He stood by the door and tapped his ear. "The house is clear."

Who the hell were these people?

Evan leaned to the side. "When I tell you to run, do it."

The mammoth by the door shook his head. "There's nowhere to run. We have the entire block blanketed."

Evan drew in a deep breath. All right. If this was his last stand, it wasn't a bad one. Then a woman walked through the doorway, and he kept his aim on the huge guy, careful not to point at her.

"Thank you, Max," she said softly, patting the big guy on the arm while carrying what looked like a doctor's bag in her free hand. She was about medium height with long black hair and stunning blue eyes, and she'd dressed in dark jeans and a light green sweater. Her smile was contagious, and those eyes really sparkled. "You must be Evan."

Tabi pushed him in the back and shoved her way to his side. "Um, hi. Your highness. I mean, Queen."

This was the queen? The woman looked like the girl next door.

"Emma," she said, her lips curving. "You demonnesses sure cause some trouble. I love that about you."

A man walked through the door, tension emanating from him. Was that charisma? Or something more? He eyed Evan and then moved to the queen's side. He was tall and broad with black hair, his eyes also shielded by glasses.

Tabi, swear to God, curtseyed. "King Dage Kayrs. I've seen pictures of you both."

King? Oh, holy crap. The woman was in deep. Evan switched his aim to this so-called king, and that Max fellow instantly growled and moved forward.

The king stopped him with a wave of his hand. "It's okay, Max. O'Connell isn't a shoot first kind of guy." He smiled, all charm. "I might've caught up on you and any records pertaining to you while we flew here. Nice job overseas, by the way." He then turned his attention to Tabi. "Tabitha Rusko. I was so sorry to learn of your guardian's passing."

Tabi gaped. "How did you know about me? About Janet?"

The king guy sighed, the sound long suffering.

Emma rolled her eyes. "He's the king. Sometimes people forget that." She turned and patted his arm. "I know you could blow up the entire world with your brain because you're so powerful and all of that, Dage, but let's stay on track here." She pressed her lips together. "So, Tabitha. You mated a human male? Fascinating." She turned and studied Evan, delight dancing across her face.

Evan had the strongest urge to step back.

Max, the massive soldier, pressed his lips together as if trying not to laugh.

Adare took in the scene from his position near door. "I'll leave you to it, then. You owe me, king." Then he smoothly walked outside and into the breezy day.

"Say hi to Grace for me," Emma called out, studying Tabi as strongly as she had Evan. "So. I was a geneticist before mating the king here, and I'm now the chief researcher for the Realm. Does anybody mind if I take a little blood?"

Evan snarled. "I have no idea what you're all into, but nobody is biting me." Did these wackos actually think they were vampires?

The queen frowned. "Biting? No. I brought syringes. Of course."

Evan calculated the odds, and they weren't good. There had been enough soldiers, fully armed, searching his house that it was possible the entire neighborhood really was covered.

Dage watched him. "Why is he so sketchy? If he agreed to mate, surely he understood the parameters."

Tabi rocked back on her heels. "Well, he might not have truly understood the situation."

Evan glanced at her, and her face turned a lovely pink. "You're wrong. I most certainly understand what's happening. You're all in some weird cult, you drugged me, and you branded my hip," he said.

The queen stood straighter. "Can I see?"

"No," Evan snapped.

Dage pursed his lips. "Let me get this straight. First, we have an enhanced male human mated by a young demonness, and second, he doesn't know about other species."

Max looked them over. "I'd say this is a clusterfuck."

Evan caught sight of the soldier's left hand. "Is that pink fingernail polish with sparkles?"

Max growled and shoved his hand in his pocket. "I lost at darts. Don't want to talk about it. Teenagers can be mean. Really, really, really mean."

Evan caught his breath. They were all crazy.

Dage shoved both of his hands in his pockets. "All right. Let's start small. Evan, I'd appreciate it if you didn't shoot me." He took off his glasses, and his eyes glowed an eerie silver.

"Nice contacts," Evan said.

Dage smiled, and fangs dropped down from his mouth.

Evan swallowed. He reacted instantly, going tense.

Dage snarled and backed away. "Jesus. That's some power. Everyone shield your minds."

Tabi nodded vigorously. "I forgot that part. He could shield before I mated him, and he even shielded me from a demon mind attack. It appears he can attack, too. The guy is talented, I'm telling you."

She actually sounded proud of him.

Evan's ears rang. "I didn't attack anybody's mind. For Pete's sakes, knock it off." How did Dage get the fake fangs? Probably some sort of movie prop.

Dage apprised him, and those fake fangs went back into his mouth. How did he do that?

Evan looked at the so-called queen. "I suppose you have wild eyes and fangs, too?"

She tapped her fingers on her doctor bag. "Of course not. I'm an enhanced human. No fangs." Her face lit and she jutted her head forward to stare at Tabi's neck. "Did he bite you, too?" She turned toward Dage. "That's interesting, right? Humans don't usually bite. We need to find more records of enhanced human males—there's so much we don't know. Even you didn't know there were any left."

Dage frowned. "I'm sure I never thought about it. Although, now remembering, I believe they could often be a threat. Something about human nature being compounded into an immortal with the male of the species."

Emma hummed. "Well, that might make sense. Enhanced females are probably more intelligent and adaptable than the male of the species. Any species." The woman didn't seem to be joking.

Dage stepped away from the queen. "It appears as if fangs and eyes aren't going to do it for you in this case, Evan O'Connell. I'm a rather busy guy at the moment, with possible wars breaking out and all of that, so let's get on with this. I guess you'd better shoot me. Aim for the shoulder or leg, would you?"

Max instantly stepped forward. "No. Shoot me."

Fuck, these folks were nuts. Evan looked at Emma, hoping for some sort of rationality.

She stepped away. "Don't shoot me. I mean, I heal as well, but I hate to get shot. It's such a pain."

Evan could feel the danger around him, but he'd never been a person who could shoot an unarmed man. He shook his head.

"For Pete's sakes." Tabi grabbed his gun, yanked it free, and shot Dage Kayrs three times in the left arm before Evan could stop her.

Chapter 9

Tabi's mouth gaped open. "I shot the king," she whispered. Who would've thought?

Dage gave her a look as blood poured from the three wounds. "Thanks for missing my head."

Evan launched into motion, grabbing a pillow from the sofa. "Press this against the wounds, and I'll call for an ambulance." His voice was low and controlled as he no doubt fell back on training.

Dage sighed and pushed the pillow away. "Watch the wounds."

"What?" Evan snapped, tension rolling from him.

"Watch," Dage said, looking down at the bleeding holes in his arm. He sucked in air, and three bullets instantly plopped out of his flesh to fall onto the wooden floor. Then the holes mended shut. He wiped his arm off, leaving streaks of blood. "All good. See?"

Evan took a step back. "But…no way. No. That was a trick."

"It was your gun, buddy." The king used the word buddy? He looked at Tabi. "You know him better than we do. If his human personality is amplified, is he dangerous?"

"No. Bossy, controlling, and protective, however," she murmured. And she'd mated the guy.

Emma smiled. "Sounds like a normal vampire to me. Now can I please take some blood? I've never studied blood from an enhanced human male or a demonness who'd just mated one. This is so exciting."

Dage lifted his chin. "I'd like him unconscious if you're near him."

Max stepped forward. "I'd be happy to knock him out."

Evan growled, low and hard. "Try it."

Desire, warm and fast, flowed through Tabi's body. That sound.

Her neck, right where he'd bitten her, pulsed as if in perfect tune. "Why don't you take my blood first?"

"No," Evan said, his back vibrating.

The queen sighed. "This is too much. Maybe they should accompany us to Realm headquarters, and we can make friends there?"

Dage crossed powerful arms, one still bloody. "I've heard worse ideas." He looked at Tabi. "How close are you to finishing with your prototypes at your factory?"

Her mouth gaped open and she quickly shut it. "How do you know—"

"The. King." Dage muttered. "I know shit. Just answer the question, please."

Very impressive. "I'm probably a couple of months out, and if those work, I can go into mass production within another couple of weeks." She tried not to sound too proud.

"Excellent," Dage said. "I hope you give the Realm the right of first refusal. We'd make it well worth your while."

She smiled. Most of her people, maybe all, really liked making money. It came in so handy for a demonness. "Of course."

Emma tilted her head. "What's your invention?"

"It's a spray that masks faces from all CCTV and other recording devices," Tabi said. "Since humans have caught up so quickly with technology, and since we potentially live for thousands of years, it's necessary."

Emma smiled. "That's brilliant. Good on you."

Tabi tried to gauge Evan's mood, but his face revealed nothing. His mind had to be spinning. "So I guess we should talk?" she asked.

He turned, disbelief still in his eyes. "I don't know what to say."

Vulnerability twittered through Tabi, and she turned toward the queen, who'd once been an enhanced human. "Was it difficult for you to accept that there were different species on the planet?"

Emma shrugged. "No, but I'm psychic and knew there was more out there than anybody else could imagine. It seems like your mate's ability is like a demon mind destroyer's. He probably didn't even realize he had an ability."

Evan shook his head wildly and then reached for his gun in Tabi's hands before placing it on the mantle. "I'm not saying I believe all of this, considering I might've been drugged last night, but if I did, are you telling me I'm about to turn into a demon?"

Max snorted. "No. Nobody turns into anything different than they started as. We're all different species. Stop watching late night television."

Evan lowered his chin in an intriguing and threatening move.

Tabi grinned. Man, he was sexy. Hopefully he wouldn't turn into an immortal jerk now that she'd forced his chromosomes to multiply. And if she believed in fate, which she might, the marking did appear on her hand after he'd kissed her. That mattered to her people. "Listen. When an immortal mates an enhanced human, the human becomes immortal and can't die except by beheading or being burned to dust. Also, mates share abilities, so that happens."

Emma nodded. "Most mates can communicate telepathically after a while, too."

Dage watched Evan closely. "Mating is forever. You touch another female, since you're mated to one, and you'll get an allergic reaction that is not funny."

Emma looked to her side at the king. "Well, mating doesn't have to be—"

"It is," Dage said, his jaw hard. "When both parties are alive, even a deadly virus won't negate the mating bond."

Emma shrugged. "That might be true." She smiled at Evan. "Welcome to immortality."

He turned and looked at Tabi. "Everyone needs to get out of my house. Except for you, Tabitha."

A shiver wound down her spine. Was it fear? No. She'd never be afraid of Evan. Maybe wary, though. Her nipples peaked.

Emma switched her bag to her other hand. "If you let me draw blood from you both, then I promise I'll take all of these soldiers out of Indiana and fly them far away. You have my word."

"I thought we were taking them to headquarters," Max interjected.

"No," Tabi said. "We have a lot going on here, but I'll contact you if we want to seek refuge." Heck. Once she told Evan everything, she might be the one needing a safe place to land. Then she placed her hand on Evan's arm and turned toward him. "Trust me. She just wants blood to study."

"Trust you?" he repeated, his gaze shuttered. "Are you insane?"

Max chuckled. "Most demons are crazy, and the Ruskos are legendary."

Tabi glowered at him.

Emma withdrew medical supplies from her bag, hopping with what looked like excitement. "Who wants to be first?"

* * * *

The atmosphere in his home did feel different after everyone had left. Evan tried to grapple with what he'd just learned and turned for his kitchen. He might as well see if he'd gone nuts.

"What are you doing?" Tabitha asked, following him.

He reached for a knife from the block. "Seeing if this is all bullshit." Taking a deep breath, he lifted the blade. It wasn't like he hadn't been cut before in a fight or two.

"Wait." She grabbed his wrist. "You probably don't have healing cells yet. Don't cut yourself."

How could he have missed an entire other world living around them? It just didn't make sense. He paused, his mind reeling.

She gently took the knife and set it on the counter. "Okay. This must seem really weird to you." For once, the woman looked unsure of herself. She sighed. "Fine." Faster than a human should be able to move, she recaptured the knife and plunged the blade through her wrist. Blood burst out of the punctured vein.

Adrenaline flooded his system so fast he leaped for the dishtowel and wrapped it around her wrist. "Tabitha," he gasped. "What the hell?"

She winced. "That really does hurt."

Blood welled through the thin material.

"Okay. Now watch." She pushed his hand away and wiped blood with the towel. The deep puncture slowly mended shut, a white scar formed, and then it disappeared into smooth skin. She twisted the faucet and washed the remaining blood off her now healed wrist.

Evan swallowed, his stomach lurching. It was all true. She was a demonness, and that didn't even mean what he'd thought it would. She was just a different species. There were different species? Fucking crazy. "I need to sit down." Before he could reach the barstool, his phone dinged from the counter, and he reached for it like a lifeline. "O'Connell."

"Detective? It's Noah Siosal, and I just returned from the store. Abby was arrested when I was gone—do you know anything about it?" The man sounded like he'd just eaten glass.

Evan straightened. "I was fired, so no doubt the sheriff is taking matters into his own hands, and he was very good friends with Abby's ex." Abby's very dead ex-husband, that was. "Do you really have lawyers outside of town?" He went into cop mode and strode through the living room for his bedroom, reaching to yank on a T-shirt and searching for his socks.

"I just called in a couple from Indianapolis, and they'll be here in about an hour," Noah said tersely. "Why were you fired?"

"Doesn't matter. Does Abby know to ask for a lawyer? I made sure the two interrogation rooms have video surveillance, so she should be okay until one arrives." Evan sat and tugged on his socks, reaching for his boots by the dresser. "I still have a couple of friends in the department and will head down there right now to make sure she's okay." He didn't put it past the sheriff to intimidate her and try for a confession.

"I'm right outside of the station. That turd threatened to arrest me if I didn't leave the premises. Get here now." Noah ended the call.

"Tabi, let the dogs inside." Evan tossed the phone on the bed and dashed into the bathroom to brush his teeth and take care of business. When he returned, Tabi was already dressed with her hair in a ponytail. He paused. Wait a minute. "Is Noah—"

She nodded. "Yep. Part vampire, part demon. He mated Abby." Tabi's black eyes lit. "Hey. You can talk to her about all the changes. Maybe you are going through the same things." She rubbed her nose. "We didn't get a chance to talk, but you have to know, if you can't get Abby out, Noah will just storm the building and damn the consequences."

Evan shoved his hair into some sort of shape. "Wait a minute. Noah and Raine are hybrids, and you're a demon? What the hell are you doing in my town and in a stupid anger-management course? You're all immortal."

Tabi blew out air. "Well, let's see. Noah was forced into it to help that Ivar dude who's gone, and then I think he stayed because of an interest in Abby. Raine was there to maybe kill that Ivar guy, and I'm not sure why he's still around. He must have a reason. And I was there because you got me on video and wouldn't give it to me until I'd successfully completed the course."

Evan shook his head. "Immortals are crazy. Batshit nuts."

"That's just not nice," she countered.

He looked at her—really looked at her. Sexy, beautiful, and

something else. Yeah. He could see it. A heat spiraled through him, landing hard in his chest and expanding out. *His.* "Before I was sick, when I was me, I was a possessive and way over-protective jackass," he rumbled.

Her eyebrows rose. "Why tell me that?"

"Fair warning," he said, a newfound power filling his body. He didn't have time to figure this new reality out right now, but whatever was going on, it started and ended with the miniature blonde looking warily at him right now.

"Hmm. Well, bottom line is that I saved your life." She tugged her wrinkled shirt into place. "We can be friends, we can be sometimes lovers, but I'm a free spirit. Don't ever forget that."

She was cute, too. He let his teeth show. "Don't think for a second that I've forgotten about Richard. Is he a demon, too?"

"Yes. You can tell by the light hair and really dark eyes. And mangled vocal cords." Her eyes flared. "I can take care of myself, Evan." A stubbornness tightened her jaw, and an impressive power flowed from her, easy to discern now that he knew more about her.

"Well now, I wasn't going to let you deal with him by yourself before I knew he was a demon." Evan strode through the living room, reclaiming his gun to tuck at the back of his waist. "You should've gotten to know me a little bit better before mating us together for eternity." The whole idea was blowing his mind, but the more he settled into it, the more he felt like himself again.

He would've never let the woman take on a powerful adversary on her own. Immortality or not.

Chapter 10

Tabi didn't mind hiding from enemies, and she enjoyed having a good fight once in a while. However, what she hated was feeling off balance. Evan had made her feel that way from the beginning, and now that she'd mated him, that sensation increased tenfold. "I really think we should talk about us and what we expect from each other," she said as he drove through town. The man had insisted on driving, and damn if she hadn't let him.

"That's fine, but right now I want to know who Richard Goncharov and the Popovs are." He turned a corner, his gaze scouting both sides of the car.

She'd forgotten he'd heard the threat from Richard. "You don't need to worry about them."

"Tabitha." One word, steel in the sound.

She rolled her eyes. "Fine. I was business partners with the Popov brothers for a while, and we didn't get along. We amicably split up our business interests. Then my developers created the spray that's going to make me billions, and the Popov brothers are pissed and out for blood."

Evan pulled into the lot of the police station. "And Richard?"

"He's very wealthy and owns a few islands. He's offered to mate me and protect me from the Popovs." Not that she needed protection, as soon as she made her own billions from the masking spray. "I'm a purebred demon, without any family, and that matters to him."

Evan frowned. "Does it matter to you?"

"No. I'm not going to mate him, and I'll handle the Popovs." She released her seatbelt.

"Oh, I don't think so." Evan cut the engine. "As I see it, you've made all the decisions so far. It's my turn."

She didn't like that at all. Her chin rose. "Now wait a—"

He was already out of the car and striding toward Noah, who waited near the front stairs of the station, looking for all the world as if he was about to storm the building.

Tabi scrambled out of the car and ran behind him, catching up just as the two males stared at each other. Why hadn't she realized how broad Evan was before?

Noah cocked his head and took them both in. "You did not."

Tabi kicked a pebble out of her way. "I did."

Evan watched him. "How can you tell?"

Noah, his eyes a blazing black, shook his head. "I can smell the change in you. In you both." He focused on Tabi. "How did you even know he was enhanced? I didn't sense anything. Didn't even know there were enhanced males around."

She swallowed. "I couldn't attack his mind, and he protected me from another attack."

"So you just went and mated him?" Noah lowered his voice. "Are you nuts? There's a reason we let enhanced human males die out." He shifted his gaze to Evan. "No offense."

"None taken." Evan turned and started climbing the steps. "You two stay out here."

Oh, she was not starting this matehood by taking orders. Tabi hustled after him. "Abby is not only my friend but my employee, and I am going to help her." Even if she had to melt the minds of everyone inside.

Evan opened the door and leaned down, his gaze hot. "Don't even think of attacking anybody. I will handle this. Got it?"

Man, he was bossy. She swept by him without answering, for the first time wondering what she'd gotten herself into. This time. "Hello." She put every ounce of charm she owned into her smile at the lone uniformed officer behind the reception desk.

The man had to be in his early twenties with wiry blond hair and a smattering of freckles that went from his forehead down his scrawny neck. He gulped. "Hi. Um, hi. Can I, um, help you?" He sat straighter in his chair and put his narrow shoulders back.

She reached the desk and leaned over, tapping her nails on the wood. "Oh, I'm sure you can, Officer...Thomas." She read his name and then focused on his eyes. "My friend was brought in here."

He swallowed loudly. "Your friend?" The man sounded like he'd really like to be her friend, too.

"Yes," she purred. "Abby Miller. Could I see her?"

The man turned red and breathed in. "Um, Abby Miller. Let me see. Um, I probably have a file here."

Evan reached her side. "Jesus. Give the kid a break, would you?" He frowned at the officer. "Barry? The sheriff arrested somebody with a solid alibi, and her name is Abby Miller. I don't want you to get in trouble, so sit here and talk to my girlfriend. I'll be right back."

Tabi's head jerked. *Girlfriend?* He'd said the word with more than a hint of possessive warning to the officer. "I'm not the girlfriend type," she retorted. She was a demon, for Pete's sake.

Evan turned, pinning her with that unreal blue gaze. Was the blue rim around his iris darker than it had been before? His chest seemed broader, too. Although he'd been pretty damn muscled before the mating. "Oh, we'll find the right term for you later, Tabitha. Right now, stay here."

A threat and an order. She'd created a monster. So she smiled, lowering her chin, and gave him a full shot of charm. "No problem." Then she winked at the furiously blushing cop. "Barry and I will just have a nice chat."

Evan's nostrils flared and he turned to stride past the desk to a wide wooden door, which he easily opened. Then he was gone.

Tabi lost the smile. Oh, that male had another think coming if he thought he was calling the shots. "Bye, Barry," she said, turning toward the outside door.

"Wait," Barry protested. "Evan said you should stay here and talk to me."

She pushed open the door, smiling over her shoulder. "Evan should learn not to give orders." Then she left the station and her new mate behind.

Jackass.

* * * *

Evan nodded at the few folks he liked and strode into the sheriff's office, slamming the door with enough force to knock a framed painting of the sheriff and his pompous family off the wall. It fell to perch on one corner of the metal frame, teetering by a scratched file cabinet.

Silence reigned outside the office, and it was telling that nobody tried to intervene. "I don't think anybody likes you," he observed, staring at the sheriff across his shiny desk.

The sheriff's pudgy nostrils flared. "What the hell are you doing here? I fired you." He stood, broad and beefy, with the window open to the quiet trees outside.

"You have one second to tell me where Abby Miller is before I call the press, Baker," Evan said, leaning back against the door. "Not just the local press, either. Those big city reporters love a small town corruption story, now don't they?" The place smelled like mothballs. Why hadn't he noticed that before? "Where is she?"

Baker's face turned a motley red color. "She's cooling it in a cell right now before I question her."

"Probable cause?" Evan barked.

"Murder. I know she murdered Monte, and I'm going to prove it. Maybe she paid those criminals in anger management to cover for her. Maybe she fucked them all. I don't know, but I will find out." Baker's eyes swirled a furious hue.

Anger settled like a cold punch in Evan's gut. "You don't have probable cause, and you know it. Not only have you harassed an innocent woman, one your buddy beat the crap out of for a year, but you've opened the county up to a lawsuit now. You're not fit for the job."

"You think you can challenge me for the job? I fired you, and doesn't that look just great?" Baker smiled, showing tobacco stained teeth. "Besides, we both know you ain't gonna be around for much longer. I've seen you shake and tremble. I saw when your leg gave out and you fell into your chair, just a couple of weeks ago. Even if you live through whatever is happening to you, you can't do this job."

"A doorknob could do this job better than you have," Evan growled, his limbs feeling like his own for the first time in years. Could he run for sheriff? Had this whole mating thing cured him, or was this just temporary? He needed to get answers from Tabitha before making any plans. Hope tried to rise in him, and he ruthlessly shoved it down. For now, he had a job to do. "Let Abby Miller out right now. Her lawyers are going to be here any minute, and from the sound of it, they'll already be planning the lawsuit." Well, probably.

Baker shifted his belt over his big belly, his eyes darting around. "I'm not out of line here."

"Wrong." Evan was done. He grabbed the keys off the hook by the door. "I'm letting her out. If you try to stop me, I will beat the absolute shit out of you in front of the other cops here. The whole town and no doubt county will hear about it, I'm sure. Yeah, I'll take a battery charge, but it'll be a first offense, and it'll hit all the papers. You know what? That might be a decent launch to a campaign for sheriff."

Baker sputtered, even his ears turning red.

Evan opened the door and strode through the bullpen to the back hallway leading to the cells. Quick movements had him at the farthest cell, unlocking the door.

Abby looked up from sitting on a blanketless cot, her greenish-brown eyes wide. She looked small and defenseless in the claustrophobia-inducing cell. "Detective O'Connell." She stood, looking over his shoulder.

"Noah is outside," Evan said, gesturing her toward him, his temper fraying. How dare the sheriff scare her like this?

Relief smoothed her features as she hurried out of the cell. "Thank goodness. I thought for sure he'd come in ripping off heads and everything." She stopped cold. "I meant that figuratively."

"Right." Evan clasped her arm and started down the hall. They probably didn't have much time before Baker found his balls and tried to stop them.

Pain ticked through Evan's palm, and he jerked away, looking at the rash on his skin. "Oh."

Abby kept walking. "Maybe you're allergic to my laundry detergent."

He opened the hallway door for her. "Or it's the mating allergy," he muttered.

She swung toward him, her jaw slack. "What did you say?"

"Later." He pointed toward the end of the bullpen, careful not to touch her again. The rash was already abating. It had appeared so quickly. Was it because they were both newly mated? Man, he couldn't believe any of this was real. "Let's get out of here."

"Good plan." She smiled serenely and nodded at the other officers, picking up her pace until she reached the door to the reception area.

The sheriff stood in his office doorway, his hands at his sides. "I'll let you go for now, Mrs. Loften. But we're not done."

Abby paused by the doorway and turned to face him fully.

Evan stopped and then waited.

"It's Ms. Miller now." She smiled. "You're a corrupt moron, Sheriff Baker. I know it, you know it, and I suspect most of the people who work for you know it. Falsely arrest me again, and I'll sue you for everything you have." She looked around at the silent officers at their desks, confidence in her gaze and her shoulders back—so much different from the woman Evan had rescued just a month before. "One of you should think about running for sheriff—if Detective O'Connell doesn't want to do so. I'll start a campaign fund right away." Then she turned and opened the door, her head held high as she exited.

Evan banked a grin and followed her through the reception area and outside, where she ran full bore into Noah Siosal's arms.

Noah grabbed her up, lifting her, inhaling her scent. "You're okay?"

She nodded. "I'm fine." When he let her down, she snuggled into his side.

Evan looked around the quiet sidewalk. "Where's Tabi?"

Noah shrugged. "She came out a while ago and drove off like hell in the BMW."

Evan's jaw set. His nostrils flared. His chest heated and his ears began to ring. "I told her to wait for me, and I believe she agreed." Oh, she had. They were about to have a serious discussion, once he found her. For now, he focused on Noah. "So. Rumor has it you're a vampire-demon hybrid."

Chapter 11

Rain started to fall as Tabi drove sedately home from her factory where the techs would work late. She was so close to mass production, and she was going to make a fortune. She glanced at her phone, which she'd left in the car all afternoon. Yep. Several calls from Evan. Too bad. He shouldn't have ordered her around earlier that day. The sooner he figured out she was her own person, the easier this transition would be for him. Hopefully Noah had given him a ride home from the station.

She shouldn't feel guilty about ditching him, so she didn't. Yet she bit her lip. The poor guy was probably really confused by this new world, and maybe she should help him out a little, considering she'd yanked him into immortality. Maybe she'd look him up in the morning.

Turning into her driveway, she stilled at seeing him leaning against her one-car garage, a badass motorcycle to the side of him.

Her panties turned wet. Plain and simple.

She swallowed and turned off the car. Okay. She could handle this. Keeping her posture ramrod straight, she stepped out of the car, grateful for the four-inch heels on her boots.

He crossed his arms, his gaze a burning blue through the dusk. "Where have you been?"

Irritation prickled up her back while heat flowed down her front. She blinked from the contrary sensations. "I was working at my factory." Not that he'd know which one was hers—there were many outside of the mainly industrial town, and she'd purchased it using several dummy corporations. "Also, you don't have the right to question me. You're no longer a detective."

"I wasn't asking as a detective," he rumbled, the rain dancing lightly over his hair.

Why was he giving her the arrogant immortal act? "You're human," she blurted out.

"I'm male," he countered, the statement firm. "Maybe human, maybe not. I don't know. What I do know is that I told you to wait for me at the police station hours ago."

She couldn't breathe. There had always been something about him, this steel hard core covered by protective instincts and kindness. "I don't take orders from you," she said, stopping a couple of feet away from him.

He cocked his head, studying her.

Tingles exploded across her skin, zipping through her body. She set her stance to hide her reaction to him. This was not going according to plan. At all.

"I had quite a nice talk with Noah today. All about vampires, demons, and the rest. All about mating and the rioting feelings that arise." His voice was low…silky. "You know what I think, Tabitha?"

Her mouth went dry. "I have no idea."

"I think you mated a human on purpose. Ambitious and independent twenty-five-year-old demonness obviously running from danger finds herself a nice human male to lead around by the nose. Have some fun and then move on, safely mated but with all the freedom in the world."

There was enough truth in the statement that her hackles rose fast. "I saved your life."

"That remains to be seen, although I have stopped shaking and feel like I could handle anything." His arms dropped to his sides. "Including you."

"That's doubtful, human." She tossed her purse back into the car and slammed the door. While only a quarter of a century old, she'd trained to fight almost from birth. If she had to beat the crap out of her new mate and show them both how this was going to go down, she'd do it. "Your stance is the wrong one. Change it." Her voice trembled just enough to piss her off even more.

He blinked. Once and slowly.

Never in her life would she have thought a blink could be threatening. Yet this was. Those blue eyes burned through the dusk, and that rim around his iris had darkened. She was sure of it. "You've lived in my world for one day, Evan. Don't think for a second you understand it," she said.

"I've lived in this world, our world, about a decade longer than you have, sweetheart. I've seen war, and I've done things for God and country that you can't even imagine." He moved then, headed her way.

For the first time in her entire life, Tabitha Rusko had to fight the urge to back *away* from danger. It was true that she'd only met the mellow detective who had thought he was at the end of his too-short life. Apparently she'd never met the soldier or the male who'd been strong enough to survive an immortal mating even while ill. He was no longer ill. What he was, she didn't know.

He reached her, standing a mere foot away. "The marking on a demon's hand only appears when their mate is near. Yours appeared when I kissed you the first time."

"Yes," she admitted. "But I don't believe in fate and all of that." Yeah, she sounded defensive and unsure.

"I do," he said, his chin down, studying her like he'd never really looked at her before. Like she was now in *his* world, and he was trying to decide what exactly to do with her.

She threw up her hands, going for a good offense. "You seemed like a laconic cop who just wanted to help people. Even though we had this obvious attraction for each other, you stayed distant. Like I plan to do." She couldn't just drop everything and trust somebody right now. Not until she set herself up with enough money and power to keep safe. Maybe to keep him safe.

"I was dying," he said, that focus becoming unnerving. "Now I'm not. Probably."

"You're not," she snapped. "Mating makes you immortal. While our blood can't cure diseases in humans, a mating does." Although he could use some doubt in his mind, apparently. She spoke too soon. Maybe she should try to reason with him, but as far as she'd heard, that rarely worked with mated immortal males. "I'm kind of on my own mission right now."

"World domination?" he drawled.

She grinned. "No. Just security and safety, which comes from money."

"I think safety now comes from me, baby." This close, power already cascaded off him—strong and sure.

Oh, crap.

* * * *

Evan hadn't felt this strong in two years. His body felt like his own again, and he studied the female in front of him intently. Interest and a barely banked vulnerability glimmered in those eyes that had haunted his dreams, and he should probably back off and let her come to terms with what they'd voluntarily done. While he had no clue what forever meant, right now, they had to come up with a plan together. The bottom line was that even though she was the immortal being, he did have years and experience on her. "You're naïve if you think money brings safety." Even he knew that.

She lifted her chin, the challenging sight stirring his desire for her even higher. "It sure doesn't hurt."

"True." The skin along his nape prickled, and he turned instinctively to see Richard Goncharov stride along the house from the backyard. Had he been waiting? Evan's chest filled and his blood flowed faster through his veins, sparking almost painfully. What was happening?

Richard, his face hard, reached the other side of the vehicle. "I've waited long enough. The Popovs are coming, and you need to leave with me now." His focus remained on Tabi, and he ignored Evan as if he wasn't there.

Evan crossed in front of the BMW, coming within a foot of the demon. "She's mated, friend. You've lost—leave town." The sense of possessiveness taking him held a life of its own—strong and brutal. He forced his hands to relax and not form fists. Whatever was happening, he would handle it like he had every other challenge in his life. "Goodbye."

Richard turned his body to face him fully, his extra inches of height making him crane his neck. "You're human."

"So I've heard," Evan said evenly.

Richard's nostrils flared in his pale face, and his eyes widened. "I smell her on you." He turned so suddenly the air cracked. "You mated a *human?*"

"Yes," Tabi said, meeting his gaze over the sports car. "It's complete and a done deal, so there's no reason for you to remain in town. I believe my mate told you to leave."

Evan settled—slightly. Hearing her claim him as her mate calmed some of the fire raging inside him. "Go."

Richard's lips peeled back and his fangs dropped. "The Popovs will kill you both. At least sell me your business—you'll have enough funds to get somewhere safe." Then he named a price that had Evan's eyebrows lifting. These people worked in millions and not thousands.

Tabi scoffed. "The business is worth billions—possibly trillions. I'll never let it go."

Evan stepped closer to the demon, not liking the fangs out. "She's safe now and will remain so." Even as a human, he would've protected her.

"You're not." Richard attacked faster than a whisper, grabbing Evan's arms and slashing sharp fangs down his neck.

Pain exploded near Evan's ear, and he shoved the demon off him.

"No!" Tabi leaped for Richard, sliding on her knees across the BMW hood, her nails scoring down his face.

The demon roared and backhanded her. The sound of his hand impacting her cheek echoed through the rain, and she cried out, tumbling backward and off the side of the car.

Anger exploded inside Evan, and he dodged forward, grabbing Richard by the neck and yanking him away from the hood with one hand, punching with the other. Richard fought back, his punches holding more strength than any human's ever had. They dropped to the ground, hitting and grappling for position.

Richard nailed Evan in the nose, and his entire skull clamored. His vision blurred.

"Stop it." Tabi jumped back into the fray, punching Richard in the neck and trying to protect Evan from the blows.

"Damn it." Evan grasped her arm to pull her out of the way.

Richard jumped to his feet and kicked Evan in the gut. Agony ripped throughout Evan's rib cage. He shoved himself to his feet, pulling Tabi up and shoving her behind him.

She pushed to his side and kicked up, nailing Richard beneath the jaw.

The demon's head snapped back, and he quickly recomposed himself, his fangs dropping even lower and his eyes swirling to a lighter gray. His reach was long enough that he swung out, smashing her right in the temple with his large fist.

She smashed into Evan's side, crying out.

Fury swelled and heated inside Evan, and he moved without thinking, punching with all his strength toward Richard's neck. His fist kept going through flesh, cartilage and bone, snapping a vertebra at the back. Growling, beyond rational thought, he swept his arm right and then left, decapitating the threat.

Richard's head dropped to the ground, rolling under the car. His body fell forward, landing on the wet pavement, his legs kicking out. Blood poured from the neck and covered the pavement.

Tabitha held her cheek and backed away, her wide eyes staring at the decapitated corpse. "You punched through his neck."

Evan stepped away, the demon's blood on his hand burning. He shook it and released the cartilage sticking to his palm. "Yeah." He came back into himself, his breath fast.

Tabi looked at him, her mouth open and shock freezing her features. "You really punched his head off."

Evan looked down at his fist. "I guess I did. I must've gotten stronger with the mating?"

She lowered her hand, revealing two large and mottled bruises forming. "You don't understand. You can't just punch through an immortal's neck. I mean, you…can't."

Evan frowned. "I did." He winced at the sight of the decapitated body. "Do demons have weak necks?"

"No." Tabi's voice trembled.

He looked at her, a cold pit settling in his gut. "Maybe Richard had some sort of neck disease?"

She slowly shook her head, watching him like *he'd* become the threat.

Huh. Evan held his hand out to let the light rain wash off the burning blood. "You've never heard of that happening?"

"Maybe during battle or in extreme duress, but only when an enemy is already on the ground," she whispered. "Nobody should be able to do what you just did. I mean, we take heads, but we usually use a sword or boot or blade. Not just a punch."

Evan sighed. "So I'm not normal."

She took another step away from him, slicing his heart in two. "No. Which means you're in more danger than we thought. We have to get rid of this body. Now."

Chapter 12

The buzzing of her cell phone awoke Tabi from a deep sleep. She reached for it before remembering where she was. A glance to the side, and she confirmed she was in Evan's bed next to the ex-cop and his incredibly hard body. Two snoring dogs sprawled out on the floor. "Hello?" she answered, trying to center herself.

"Hi, Tabi. It's Emma. I'm sorry to have awakened you," the queen said, sounding distracted.

Tabi sat up, her breath catching. "That's all right. What's going on?"

"Nothing. I just finished the blood tests, and your blood is reacting like any new mate's would. Evan's is different, but I think it's just because he's the only enhanced human male I've ever tested. The cells are wild, really. How is he doing?"

"Great," Tabi said. "How is his blood different?"

Evan turned on his side, his blue eyes clear as he watched her.

"His blood is changing much faster than I've ever seen a mate's blood change, which might be unique to him, rather than all human males. The cells are amping up like they've been shot full of adrenaline, and the chromosomal pair advancement is almost already done. I just don't know. He might be stronger than most immortals as well, but we'll see. I assume he'll be like most mates and gain your skills, but his might be enhanced on their own, which would be something new. I'd like to conduct more tests on him."

Tabi swallowed. "We'll definitely keep it in mind."

"Is he showing any unusual signs? Anything that has caught your attention?" the queen asked.

"Well, he's being a bossy and overbearing butthead," Tabi said, remembering the night before when he hadn't really given her a choice in where she was staying the night. "I'd even say controlling."

Emma laughed. "That's not out of the ordinary for a mate. I meant something more or that doesn't seem right."

Like the fact that Evan had punched right through a demon soldier's throat the night before and then had calmly dug a grave in the middle of nowhere that would never be found? "No, I haven't noticed anything," Tabi lied. "If I do, I'll call you right away. For now, we have some adjusting to do."

"I understand. It's not an easy time for a new mate, even one who's a demonness. Take it from somebody who's been there. Life is a lot easier if you work together on it, and being protected and safe is a pretty nice way to live—especially once you have kids." The queen signed off.

Kids? Who said anything about kids? Tabi was at least a century away from wanting kids, and if Evan was this overbearing now, he'd be impossible once they had kids. If they had kids. If they stayed together to have kids someday in the far away future, which was something she had not agreed to yet.

She looked over at her mate. After disposing of the body the night before, Evan had insisted she stay the night at his bungalow, and she'd basically passed out from exhaustion and what was probably shock.

In the early dawn light, he watched her in that way he had—one he'd used even as a human. Now it held even more power.

Her body short-circuited in response, one more thing out of her control suddenly. Rain splattered against the window, with the storm having strengthened throughout the night, and her blood started to pump in tune with the wild weather. "Your tests show you might have a very rare extraordinary strength," she murmured.

"No kidding." He continued to watch her.

She met his gaze, refusing to back down. "If you have something to say, say it."

"If I'd met you when I was healthy, I would've handled you differently," he said, his voice a low rumble in the morning.

She partially turned to face him, comfortable that the borrowed shirt covered her completely. "Handled me? I don't think so, Detective."

He leaned up on his powerful arm, and the muscles rippled across his chest. "I was trying to save you from the hypocrisy in this town, in this county, so you could leave before I died."

She forced a smile, hoping it looked somewhat bored. Or sarcastic.

"You're done trying to save me now?"

One of his dark eyebrows rose. "Oh, I'm definitely going to save you from whoever these Popovs are, and we're going to have a nice long talk about them later today. I want to know everything, and if there's a way to reason with them without killing, I'll find it."

"And if not?" she whispered.

His gaze didn't waver. "Then I'll take off their heads." He looked down at his other fist. "Apparently I don't need any other weapon to do so."

Just because he'd been able to decapitate one demon that way didn't mean he could do it again. Maybe this bizarre strength was temporary as his body completed the mating to become immortal. "Listen, Evan. I'm not sure what's happening to you and how you're changing, but I think we need to set a couple of parameters here."

Was that amusement in his eyes? "Interesting. Tell me how I'm changing."

She'd wanted to talk about parameters, but maybe they should discuss this. "I don't really know, but it seems like new 'immortal pain-in-the-ass' testosterone, or whatever male demons or vampires have, is flooding you and changing you a bit. I'm sure it will abate." She hoped. Forget the fact that it was sexy and intriguing. She'd better set him straight now.

"Hmm." He ran his free hand down her arm, the touch electrifying. And possessive. "Different theory. The illness I had as a human changed me, and now that I'm getting healthy, and believe me, I feel healthy again, maybe I'm going back to my default setting. This is the real me, Tabitha."

"I'm not certain what that means," she admitted, acutely aware of the strength he now possessed as well as the fact that they were in bed together. Intimacy wound around them, through her. She swallowed, trying to hide the sudden sense of vulnerability.

"You never have to fear me. I promise." He tugged her down and rolled on top of her, heat and male pressing her to the mattress and stealing her breath. "I understand that we're both in new worlds all of a sudden, and we can navigate it all together. But you need to understand, I'm not relenting on this one fact. We are a team, and that's how we'll proceed forward."

"A team has a leader," she said, her gaze dropping to his mouth.

"We can divide the tasks," he said, grinning. "I remember the early days before my mom passed away, and my parents created a plan together. She handled school and he handled sports. She handled health and church, and he dealt with the money. They worked well together."

She blinked. "That sounds like a good family. I'm sorry you lost them."

His face softened. "You are a sweetheart sometimes. You don't have family?"

The idea hurt. "No. There's nobody."

"Wrong. There's me. You and me." He kissed her forehead, his lips heated. "Are you mine, Tabi?"

Whoa. Wow. "Um." A jolt of awareness and want took her by surprise. His? Her thighs softened. "This isn't turning out like I thought." Yeah, her voice went hoarse and needy, and her core started to ache. For him. Only for Evan O'Connell, a male it appeared she couldn't control.

His grin held steel. "I figured. Why don't you tell me what you'd planned?"

That was the problem. She never planned—or hardly ever. "Well, I guess I thought you'd be grateful I'd saved your life and then I'd kind of protect you from afar and do my thing." It was difficult to concentrate with his hard body over her.

He shifted his weight, settling his rigid cock between her legs. Only the thin material of her panties separated them. She bit back a moan.

By the flaring of his eyes, he felt it against his chest. "Is that how things usually go with immortals?"

She snorted. "No. Not at all. Didn't you notice that either Dage or Max could've taken both of us out if either of us had threatened Emma? I'm sure the queen can fight, and I'm also sure the queen has never needed to fight." She paused. "But—"

"No but. I've had more fighting experience than you have, and it appears I'm stronger." He frowned, for the first time losing the arrogant glint in his eyes. "We're going to have to watch that and make sure I can control it. I'd never want to hurt you. Or anybody else, really."

Relief swamped her. Evan was back. The one she knew. "I agree, and I'm willing to stay here until you feel comfortable with your new powers. We'll work on it until you're sure you've got it under control."

"Tell me about the Popovs so I can handle them," he said.

Damn it. The Evan she'd known was *so* not back. "I'll handle them."

He brushed his nose across hers, both hands sliding her camisole up her ribcage. "If I haven't been clear, I apologize. You are no longer handling anything by yourself."

The thrill that took her was because of his warm hands and not the thought that she wasn't alone. That this big, strong, badass of a gentle giant was now being a bossy asshat should not turn her on or make her happy.

Yet the warmth in her center wouldn't leave. "Evan—"

"You haven't answered my question, so I'll lead you there." He removed her top, settling his bare chest over hers and groaning softly. "Are we mated?"

She rolled her eyes, her hands working on their own to caress down his flanks. Her nipples hardened against him. "Yes."

"Is mating forever?"

"Apparently so," she said, scratching down his heated back, still sure she could turn this around. "You're welcome for my bringing you into this world."

"Hmm." He kissed her then—finally. Deep and sure with more than a hint of power. Oh, it had been there before, but he'd held back. Now he gave it all, giving her no choice but to take it. Then he released her, leaning back as if time had no meaning. "I was already in this world but hadn't realized how big it was. Now you're with me in it, demonness. I'm being as gentle as I can be with you, but you're going to come to grips with it and soon."

How had she missed this in him? "What the hell does that mean?" Why was he turning her on and pissing her off at the same time? It was too hard to concentrate.

"You mated me knowing full well what mating meant. I'm just taking you up on the offer." His phone buzzed and he stiffened, reaching for it on his dresser. "It's the king."

She stiffened. "The king has your cell number?"

"Yeah. I called in a favor before he left the other day." Evan sounded so damn casual about the freaking king of the entire Realm.

Who was this male she'd mated? What had she done? "What favor?"

"I let his woman take my blood and yours." Evan lifted the phone. "Morning, Dage. What do you have?" His voice was all business, and then he listened, his gaze remaining on Tabi's eyes. "When?" Those blue eyes narrowed. "Thanks for arranging the meeting." He ended the call, his jaw hardening.

"What?" Tabi whispered.

The phone shattered in his hand. He looked at it, his brows rising. "Shit."

She shivered, taken aback. Maybe he was more dangerous than even she'd realized. "We need to work on that strength."

He tossed the useless pieces toward the floor and looked back at her. "*We.* I like that. Now you're learning."

Irritation mixed with the desperate desire flooding her. This entire situation had gotten away from her, and it seemed Evan had the control now. Oh, she had to do something about that but couldn't think of the right move. "What did the king say?" she asked.

"The Popovs flew to Indiana yesterday. They're here now." He rolled off her to stand.

She sat up, grabbing the covers. Wait a second. They had been getting naked and working out this dynamic between them. Hopefully an orgasm or two would get them on the same track. "What the heck are you doing?"

"I'm going to take care of them. One way or the other. You stay here." He reached for his discarded jeans.

She jumped out of bed, not caring she was only wearing light green panties. "Oh, hell no."

Chapter 13

The Popovs weren't what Evan expected. He sat across from them at Jimmy's diner in the middle of town, their table at the rear of the local landmark. They were brothers, and they looked like it. What they didn't look like were demons.

Allen seemed to be the leader of the two, and his black hair was longer than his brother's and reached his shoulders. He also looked to be an inch or two taller. Both males had reflective topaz colored eyes and a lot of facial hair that wasn't exactly groomed. Did some demons look like hicks?

Tabi sat next to him, her expression serene but her eyes lively. "Heard you two had some trouble down in Argentina with your factories."

The younger brother, Lance, leaned forward. "That was you?"

She waved her delicate hand through the air. "Of course not. You know that's not my style. Although I wouldn't be surprised if it had been Richard Goncharov in an attempt to woo me."

Allen snorted. "I heard about that. Apparently you didn't take him up on the offer, and yet I'll track him down about those factories. Thanks for the tip."

"He's dead," Evan said smoothly.

Lance looked at Tabi. "You?"

"No," Evan said. "Me."

The two males turned to study him, although they'd been unobtrusively doing so since Evan and Tabi had sat in the still busy café.

"You're not a vampire or demon," Lance said quietly.

"Neither are you," Evan said.

Tabi jumped. "Didn't I tell you? Sorry. They're wolf shifters."

Wolf fucking shifters? People who actually turned into animals? That only happened on television. How many other species were in the world, anyway? Evan kept his face stoic and his questions at bay. So many questions. "My mate forgets to fill in details sometimes."

Tabi stiffened. "I've been busy."

Allen's eyebrows lifted. "Stealing from other people instead of just us these days, have you?"

Evan kept the male's gaze. "Tabi? Did you steal from these folks?"

"No." She hopped on her chair, irritation wafting from her that ticked up his spine. Interesting, his body reacted to her emotions, and his hand closed into a fist. "We ended our arrangement before my techs discovered the best prototype," she finished.

Oh, there was no doubt the female had ended the partnership at an opportune time, but as far as Evan was concerned, that was business. "Well, then. What is it you gentlemen want?"

Lance tilted his head. "Not a shifter or witch. I've got it. You're a fairy."

Fairy? Evan frowned.

"Yep. He's Fae," Tabi agreed. "Most people can't sense it. Nice job, Lance."

Fae? Yet another freaking species? What was that about witches? Man, Evan needed to get caught up on this world. Why had Tabi lied? Apparently it was less dangerous for him to be thought of as a Fae than an enhanced human male. Was he really that deadly? Maybe it wasn't safe to be around him, but he'd always had skills, and he'd tempered them. Could he do so now? "All right," he muttered. "Let's get to it, then."

Allen gazed at him. "I heard your people can no longer travel between worlds. That must suck."

Worlds? What worlds? Evan's patience was rapidly shredding. Being in the dark was never a good position. Apparently he needed to sit his smart-ass mate down and get more answers about pretty much everything. "Let's keep to the subject. What. Do. You. Want?"

Allen blinked. "Half ownership of any company with a stake in the new masking spray. I know you're close, Tabitha."

"No," she said smoothly.

"We won't take anything less," Lance said. "Make the agreement, or you'll be looking over your shoulder for the rest of your probable short life." His eyes swirled, looking nothing close to human. "It'd be a pity for you to lose your new mate so quickly, Tabitha."

Evan leaned forward. "The only thing that saves you from a quick death is that you threatened me and not her." He'd never fought a shifter before. "Asking for half of the business is ridiculous, and you know it." He looked to his mate at his side. "Is there any agreement you'll reach?" If she said no, then they might as well forget lunch. He took a drink of his coffee, letting her think it out. This was her business and her decision.

She sat back, calculation crossing her features that was probably the sexiest thing he'd ever seen. Smart girls had always knocked him out, and this one was brilliant and cunning—and a little reckless. He could temper the last one so she didn't get hurt. She twirled her coffee cup. "Well, I suppose we could reach a new deal."

Allen sat back, distrust darkening his eyes. "Go on."

"In order to mass produce the spray, I'm going to need several more facilities in the form of production and distribution. You have an excellent pipeline throughout most of the world. You pay me ten billion dollars so I can create the production facilities, and we use your distribution channels."

"Sure," Lance said. "For sixty percent of the company."

"Twenty," Tabi said, sipping calmly.

God, she was magnificent. Evan sat back to just watch her work, his chest expanding. From day one, she'd fascinated him. The first time he'd kissed her, he'd sank into home. Every new facet of her was fascinating...and his.

Allen laughed. "Not a chance, demonness. We'll give you no money up front but use our production and distribution systems for half the company. Forever."

"No," she said, finishing her drink. "My production facilities, because I don't trust you not to steal the invention. In my position, you wouldn't, either. Ten billion up front, and you get a thirty percent interest in the company. That's my final offer, and you have until tomorrow morning to decide. After that, I go another avenue." She pushed back her chair and stood.

Evan followed suit, leaving money on the table for all of the coffee. "Thank you, gentlemen." He pressed a hand to the small of his mate's back and escorted her from the restaurant, acutely aware of the different atmosphere from the shifters. Hot and angry.

Furious.

* * * *

Tabi held her head up high as she slipped into the passenger side of her own car. "I don't see why you have to drive."

He sat and looked at her, starting the engine. "You drive too fast. Way too fast."

"I like speed," she protested.

"Yeah, well this is a peaceful place with kids who don't look both ways before chasing a ball across a street," he countered, driving out into the quiet main drag.

There was the small town cop she'd crushed on from day one. Thinking of kids chasing baseballs. How was he the same guy who'd dug a grave the night before? "Are you okay about last night?"

He slowed down to let two elderly ladies cross the street toward the Eagles' Lodge. "Yes."

"I'm talking about killing someone and then burying his body— outside of the law." Had she ruined him?

He stopped at the one stop sign in the town, turning to look at her. Full on, blue stare. "He threatened what's mine. He threatened you. I'm absolutely fine with him no longer being a threat."

Whoa. Oh boy. Okay. "Is this a new thing, since we mated?" Maybe she should call the queen.

"I was a sniper for a SEAL Team before becoming a detective here as I prepared to die, sweetheart. I don't like killing, but I will protect my country and now you, with whatever means are necessary." His broad hands were more than capable on the steering wheel, and the muscles in his forearms flexed nicely. At least he hadn't broken the car yet.

She studied him. Strong and capable. He was dressed in a dark T-shirt with faded jeans, filling out both with ripped muscles. His body was impressive, and there was no doubt he was intelligent. But his heart, the protective way he had of caring for the people in the town, was what had caught her eye. Even though she'd been in trouble after beating the crap out of those boys who'd tried to mess with her, he'd been sweet and had helped her through the court system.

Her heart warmed.

He took another turn, heading back to his house. "Since we're talking billions here, how much is enough? Why not go into business with these guys?"

"They're jerks, and you can never have enough. It's the only way to stay safe," she countered.

"You mated me. That's your way to stay safe," he said, his voice way too calm.

She couldn't think. He was sounding more like an immortal than ever, and now what was she going to do? "Money is good, too."

"Maybe. You hungry? We didn't get breakfast."

There he was again, making sure she was all right. It was decent that he'd changed the subject, too. She jumped on it. "Yeah. I don't suppose you can cook."

His grin flashed quick and smooth. "You haven't lived until you've had my blueberry pancakes. I'm about to make you very happy."

The promise went deeper than that, and she could almost touch it. So she backed away. "I'm not one for sharing."

"You'll learn."

She blinked. "What I'm trying to say—"

"I know what you're trying to say," he said, pulling into his driveway. "You've been alone for a long time and you've never relied on anyone. Especially a man. I'll give you time to work through it, Tabi. But I won't let you run, so get that out of your head right away." Even with the threat, his voice remained soft and kind—with absolutely no give.

"If I ran, you wouldn't find me," she challenged.

"Want to bet?" he asked.

Definitely. Oh, she couldn't run right now with her factory, but someday, they were going to play that game. It hit her then. She had started planning with him. How had he done that? Her mind spinning, she stepped out of the car and didn't feel the threat until it was too late.

A multitude of darts impacted her side, shooting down her legs. "Evan," she whispered, trying to turn and see him.

His roar of raw fury sounded more animalistic than anything she'd ever heard. So many darts showed on his face and down his torso that she couldn't count them all. The blue of his gaze, primal and desperate, was the last thing she saw before the darkness pulled her down.

It swirled around her, while nausea rippled through her stomach. The ground was hard and the rain soft. Grunting, she flipped all the way to her back, letting the cool droplets plaster her face and along her body.

She couldn't move her hands or feet. The hum of her vehicle, still running, competed with the rustling wind and strengthening rain.

Good. The stronger the storm, the better.

The drugs from the darts coursed through her body, rendering her limbs useless and her mind fuzzy. Darkness swam in from the edges of her brain, and she fought hard to remain semi-conscious.

Her temples pounded like she'd been punched as her body tried to diffuse the drugs.

Where was Evan? She could only hear the BMW and the rain storm. Finally, she could wriggle her fingers. Then her toes. Preparing for the pain, she blinked open her eyes.

Even though the day was cloudy, the light pierced right to her brain in sharp agony. She moaned and rolled to her side, gagging several times but keeping the coffee down. How long had she lain there? Slowly, painfully, she pushed to sit, accidentally knocking her head against the passenger side door. "Evan?" she called.

Only the rain and the engine echoed back. She pulled the darts out to drop on the ground.

Heaving, her stomach rolling, she curled her hands over the tire and pulled herself to stand. She staggered around the front of the car, balancing herself by holding on to the hood. She reached the other side and found rainy cement. No Evan.

She shook her head, trying to focus. It took three times for her to be able to open the driver's door, and she flopped into the seat, twisting the ignition off.

A note was stuck to the steering wheel. Taking a deep breath, she slowly unfolded it, her hands shaking. As she read, she forced bile back down her throat. Tears filled her eyes—either from pain or fear, she wasn't sure. The note was short and to the point.

The Popovs had Evan, and they'd cut off his head within sixty minutes if she didn't bring the prototype to them. She looked at the clock.

The note had been left more than an hour ago.

Chapter 14

Evan awoke face down on a dirt floor. He turned his head and coughed out dust before sitting up.

"Hello, Sleeping Beauty," came a low voice.

Evan shook his head, trying to remember where he was. Back in Afghanistan? He couldn't concentrate. His stomach lurched, and he rolled to the side, coming up to his knees and then his feet. He swayed but remained standing in a perfectly square metal cell—the box kind that's moveable. He wiped dirt out of his eyes and focused to see Lance Popov on the other side. "Where's Tabitha?"

"We took you and not her," Lance replied.

So he was bait. Good to know. "Why the dirt in this metal cell?" he muttered, his teeth crunching dirt he must've inhaled.

Lance sat on a folded chair in what appeared to be a vacant warehouse. "It has molecules of planekite in it, just in case. I didn't think you were a witch, but it never hurts to be sure."

"Planekite?" he asked before his brain kicked back in. Crap. He probably should know what that was. Grunting, he pulled out the darts to flick toward the shifter.

Lance rolled his eyes. "I know there are several names for the mineral, but we call it planekite. You know what I'm talking about." He cocked his head. "Or don't you? I guess if you're Fae, you have probably been off world for a long time? Until recently, anyway."

What the hell did 'off world' mean? Evan moved to the bars of the cell. "Right. Off world. So—planekite?" He couldn't quite manage full sentences yet.

"It's a mineral that weakens and ultimately kills witches," Lance said. "Guess you're not a witch."

"Guess not." However, hadn't somebody said that enhanced humans were related to the witches? Nobody had sounded sure. He was feeling weak and his blood was flowing sluggishly, but he'd also been darted pretty heavily. "What was in those darts?" They'd pierced his skin easily enough.

Lance chuckled, the sound echoing around the empty room. There were two large doors and bays, so this was probably storage for vehicles or maybe boats? "Those darts held enough sedative to take down a cadre of vampires. You should still be out and in lala land. I guess you crazy fairies have some gifts I hadn't heard about."

"Guess so." Hopefully enhanced human males had even more gifts. Evan planted his hands on the bars to test their strength. Solid. Pretty solid. "What's your play here?"

Lance tugged a knife with a jagged edge out of the sheath in his right boot. "Your mate is bringing the prototype here to trade for your life. It's pretty simple."

"Is it?" Evan drawled, his faculties slowly returning.

Lance grinned. "Well, maybe not. Your mate is a lying bitch, even for a demonness, so we're going to get the prototype and kill you both once she arrives. If she arrives. Think she'll come for you?"

Evan tightened his grip around one of the bars. "I think it's interesting your brother isn't here." Tension rolled through him followed by a healthy dose of anger. "Where is he?"

"You're not as dumb as you look," Lance observed. A phone trilled, and he tugged one from his front pocket with his free hand. "Lance." Then his eyebrows lifted and he looked at Evan. "No shit. Guess you won that bet. See you soon." He ended the call. "The bitch is on her way here. Guess she does have a feeling or two for you."

"That's the last time you call her a bitch, Lance," Evan growled, the energy beginning to run through his veins again. "Where is your brother?"

Lance twisted the knife, staring as it reflected light around the room. "He followed her to the factory. We couldn't find it, you know. The female is a master at using dummy corporations." He flipped the knife up and caught the handle on the way down. "I have wanted to cut her for so long."

Evan snarled, his chest widening. He stood taller. Her image flashed through his mind, giving him more strength. Tabi. His Tabi. He should've told her how he felt about her, even though it didn't make a lick of sense that it had happened so quickly. Instead, he'd just bossed her around. Not that she didn't need a little bit of protection and sense. "You're not going to touch her."

"Oh, but I am," Lance said, twirling the knife again. "Who knew that she'd lose this game over a mate? I didn't think she had it in her to care."

"So you darted us and then your brother followed her to find the factory—just in case she didn't come for me." As a plan, it didn't suck. Tabi was smart. She had to know she was walking into a trap. "She won't come for me. Your brother is mistaken."

The door opened and Tabi strode inside, holding a medium-sized light blue box. "Wrong." Her blonde hair was long down her back, and she wore black jeans with those deadly heels giving her additional height. She looked at him, her black eyes glittering. "You okay?"

Allen walked in behind her, a green gun in his hand and a wary light in his eyes. "This was too easy."

Evan pulled on the bar, his hand slipping off. "What the hell are you doing here?"

She shrugged. "I couldn't just let them kill you." One of her light eyebrows arched.

He subtly shook his head. So far, the bar hadn't moved. Either his super strength was gone, or the bars were fortified even against such power.

She sighed. "Well. This is unfortunate."

Man, she was cool under pressure. Or maybe she didn't realize that their situation actually sucked. "What's in the box, Tabitha?" Evan asked quietly.

Her grin was catlike. She tugged out a black remote control.

Allen pointed the gun at her. "What is that?"

She pressed a button, and an explosion rocked the entire county.

Evan dropped his head. "Please tell me you didn't just blow up your factory."

"There was nobody inside, Evan. Give me some credit." She threw the box toward Lance. "I went inside to make sure the place was clear. See how you're influencing me already?"

Influencing her? Considering he was in a cell and she was outside of it with two maniacal shifters, he wasn't getting through to her. "I'd really appreciate it if you wouldn't walk into danger like this."

Allen fired the green gun toward the high roof. Green lasers zipped out and apparently turned into metal when hitting the interior metal of the roof. Shards rained down, all around him, and he didn't so much as flinch. He then pointed the weapon at Tabitha. "Where is the formula?"

She tapped her head. "Right here, jackass. It's the only place, you know. I created it."

Lance stood to face her. "So we need your head and not your mate's. Okay."

"Nope," she said, widening her stance. "I'm a demonness. You can't torture me for information. He goes, and I go, and we'll make an agreement. I'll give you half of the company in exchange for your distribution channels. The labs remain mine."

Evan reared up. "You are not giving in to blackmail."

She waved a hand. "This is normal business practice in my world."

Great. Just freaking great. "I don't think kidnapping me should earn them fifty percent of your business, honey. It's rewarding bad behavior," Evan drawled, looking for a way out of the cell.

Surprise flashed in her eyes. "I thought I'd find you a little more freaked out. Maybe your time in the military prepared you better than I'd thought."

At least she was finally seeing him. "Why are you here? Why come yourself?" He had to know.

She sighed. "Fine. I like you. Have since the beginning. You're hot and strong and kind. Maybe a little bossy. Definitely sexy."

"Just like me? Only like?" he asked, releasing his hold on the bars.

Allen cleared his throat. "Do you two mind? We're in the middle of something here."

"Right." Tabi lowered her head. "I guess I'll just fry your brains." Power shot from her, nearly visible.

Allen immediately yelled in pain, blood spurting from his ears.

Lance leaped between them, taking the hit. He screamed.

Allen dropped to the floor, using his brother as a shield. He leaned around his writhing brother and fired several times toward Tabi.

Evan bellowed a warning.

Bullets hit her and she went down, her eyes wide as blood spurted from her torso. Agony darkened her expression. "Well, shit," she muttered.

* * * *

Pain blew through Tabi's chest and she cried out, trying to breathe. She might've overestimated her ability to take on both shifters with her mind. As her body rushed to heal itself, her brain slowed down with the demon mind attack. She'd been so intent on saving Evan that she hadn't thought of the consequences. Not at all.

Whimpering, she shot out another mind attack, trying to remain conscious.

Allen stood and fired again. Blood burst from her leg a second before the pain jolted her system.

A savage roar bellowed from the cage, the sound so primal that everyone froze. She gasped and turned to see Evan grab above the bars and swing his legs, kicking two bars out. Then another two. They shot across the empty warehouse, dropping to the concrete and bouncing away with loud tings.

He moved faster than a blur, right at Allen, who pivoted and fired several lasers at Evan.

Tabi cried out and tried to sit, sending healing cells where she could. Blood continued to pour from her.

Evan impacted Allen, taking him down to the concrete. Blood and dirt coated the way he'd traveled. The gun spun away, smashing into the broken cell.

Tabitha scrambled toward it along with Lance, both of them fighting to reach the weapon.

Allen shrieked, the high decibels reaching every corner of the warehouse. Tabi paused, shaking, turning to see Evan lift the shifter's head up and throw it into the cell. Allen's hair caught on the broken bars, and his head hung there, swinging back and forth.

Lance swung his entire body around and kicked the gun to fly yards away. Yelling, he lowered his head.

Tabi leaned up. "Run, Evan! He's going to shift. Now!" The percussions sent out might kill them both.

Evan stood and turned, blood coating his chest.

Lance's arms and legs stretched out, and fur emerged all over his face.

Evan leaped over him, landing next to Tabi, and rolled her across the floor. Ripples spread around them and a crash echoed. Evan stopped them yards away, planting his body over hers and covering her head to toe.

The air exploded, sucking in and then out. The force pulled Evan off her, and he fought to cover her, tucking his head over her neck.

Then silence.

She gasped and looked over to see a fully formed wolf.

Evan shoved to his feet, positioning himself between Tabi and the animal. "Holy shit, he's big," he muttered. "Bigger than any wolf."

The animal snarled, saliva dripping from its razor sharp canines.

Tabi planted one bloody hand on the cement and forced herself to stand. She wobbled. "He's much stronger in this form."

Evan's back was covered in blood, too. Had the bullets gone all the way through? He sucked in air, pain cascading off him. "Get out of the way, Tabitha." He staggered forward, pushing her behind him with one dirty hand still dripping with Allen's blood.

Tabi elbowed him in the side. "I've got this." She lowered her chin, but before she could send out an attack, the wolf leaped through the air.

The animal hit them both, sending them sprawling across the cement floor. Tabi smashed her head on the wall, and lights flashed behind her eyes just as the bone in her wrist snapped in two. She yelped.

The wolf growled and jumped for her.

Evan careened off the floor and wrapped both arms around the wolf's body, tackling the beast to the cement. They landed hard, both scrambling for purchase. The wolf raked sharp claws down Evan's arm, and he bellowed, punching rapidly toward the animal's throat.

Grunting, swearing, Evan scissored his legs around the wolf, trapping it. Then he punched the animal between the eyes, his fists too fast to track.

The wolf snarled and snapped its teeth, aiming for Evan's neck.

Evan swore and grabbed the wolf's jaw with both hands, yanking in the opposing directions. The bone dislocated with a loud snap, and the animal yipped. Evan kept going, tearing the head in two. The body shuddered, furry and bloody, into death.

Holy crap. Tabi turned and coughed, trying not to throw up.

Evan hitched toward her, leaning down. "Like me? You only like me?"

She tried to answer, but everything hurt. "We need to heal ourselves." She pulled him to sit next to her while also sending healing cells to her wrist. The bone popped back into place, and she jumped.

His eyebrows rose. "Okay."

She took a deep breath. "Imagine your injuries and send healing cells to them. Close your eyes. You can do it."

He followed her orders. "We're not done talking, mate." Then the cut on his forehead healed much faster than any new mate's should.

It figured.

Chapter 15

The storm continued outside while Evan finished showering, letting the heated water get rid of all the blood and dirt. He looked at his chest. Oh, the scars from his time in the military were still there, but no recent bullet holes. Not a one. He should feel good about that.

Right now, something was driving him. Something deep and uncomfortable. He didn't regret killing the Popovs, because those two would've never stopped coming for Tabi and her company. While he didn't give two fucks about the company, she did, so that mattered. More importantly, she mattered.

He flipped off the water and stepped out of the steam, drying off. Power sang through him, even more so after the fight. Was that normal? Maybe it was just normal for him. He'd have to figure this whole immortal thing out and deal with this bizarre strength, but that was second.

First was waiting for him in his living room because he'd told her to wait there. After her shower.

He stalked into his room, not surprised to see both dogs on his bed. He gave them a look and drew up clean jeans, not bothering to button them. Then he padded barefoot into the living room and finger combed his hair as he went.

Tabi sat on the sofa, dressed in his faded Metallica T-shirt with a blanket over her knees. "Feel better?"

"No." He paused, looking at her. God, she was beautiful. Strong and smart and fragile and spunky. An entire package, and she'd only lived a sliver of her long life. What would she be like in a hundred years? A thousand? Everything inside him wanted to know. Wanted to be there. But there had to *be* a there. "You will never walk into danger like that again." The words were out, and he let them hang in the air.

She paused in her perusal of his healed chest. "They had you in a cell."

"I got out of the cell," he countered.

She plucked a string on the blanket. "How did I know you could get out of a cell?"

"Again, that doesn't matter. What you know or don't know—don't ever walk into a trap like that. You're smart, Tabitha. You knew it was a trap." More importantly, she had to learn to trust him. He could take care of himself, even in this new world. "Yet you came—with a fucking light blue box from a jewelry store."

"It was an extra box," she said, all sass.

"Watch it, baby," he warned, wanting to go gentle since it had been a shitty night. "I like your sass usually. Not so much right now."

Her eyes flared and warmed. Yeah, she liked it when he called her *baby*. She equally didn't like being told what to do. He knew both facts about her, because her feelings all but danced across her pretty face. "Please. I knew one of them wanted to follow me to and from my factory to find it. Yet I figured I could get you free. Didn't know you could break bars," she muttered.

"You blew up your factory for me." The idea warmed him, while the sight of her bloody on the ground chilled him at the same time.

She shrugged. "Yeah. You're more important than a factory."

Now she was trying to charm him? It was working. "How far behind does this put you?"

Her body visibly relaxed as they turned to business talk. "Only a month or two. I know the recipe, and the techs are mine, so we just need to get another production facility up and running. And buy the ingredients, of course."

"Good. Have you ever seen shifters do that before?"

She nodded. "Sure."

He licked his bottom lip. "So you knew about the percussion wave created when one of them shifted near you?"

She moved uneasily on the sofa, sliding to stand. "Well, kind of."

"Tabi?" His voice softened, and she was smart enough to catch it. "What happens to a demon mind attack when a shifter turns into a wolf?"

She swallowed. "I don't think that's really—"

"Tabi." He waited. Not so patiently.

"Fine. When a shifter turns to the animal form, most often, a demon mind attack no longer, er, works." Then she rolled her eyes.

Mistake. Big one.

* * * *

Nerves jumped inside Tabi's belly. So she rolled her eyes.

He came at her then. Full on, right for her. She was a second late in identifying the vibe in the room as scary, pissed-off immortal. She swallowed and sidled around the coffee table.

He stopped. One eyebrow rose.

She moved a little more, edging toward the kitchen.

"Where are you going?" he asked, his voice gravelly and low.

"Thirsty?" If she could just get some air, she could figure this out.

"No." He clocked her progress, looking big and bad and pretty damn sexy. "You done trying to make a run for it?"

It was one of her skills. "You're in a mood." One that was having the interesting result of heating her abdomen and softening her thighs. What was it about him?

"Good of you to notice." He tracked her then, sure and strong steps.

She backed away, her heart thundering, her body healed. "What are you doing?"

"Settling things." He reached her, his scent of smoke and honey wafting along her skin.

She took another step back, caught between the wall and his body. If she could just slide to the right, she could reach the kitchen. Although the broad spanse of his ripped chest all but begged for her mouth.

As if reading her mind, he planted a hand on the wall by her head, caging her. Easily. "I'd like to give you another chance to respond to my statement that you do not just breezily walk into danger that *does not* include you rolling your eyes." While his voice was soft, his eyes were intense, and his body vibrating.

She couldn't have rolled her eyes if her life depended on it. Plus, breezily hadn't exactly described her actions. "I guess I could agree to those conditions." Her lungs seemed to be fighting her.

"No more danger, Tabitha."

She shivered from the heat in his eyes. Human, her ass. He was all immortal badass. "Danger isn't my thing." She tried to sound agreeable.

He traced his free hand along her jaw and down her front, between her breasts. "Right. You go into business with shifters, and you double-cross them."

She gasped.

Now he rolled his eyes. "Please."

Okay. Her grin even felt sassy. "No more business arrangements with shifters."

"Good. No more beating up humans, either." His fingers were gentle as he lifted the shirt over her head, baring her to him.

She shrugged. "Whatever. I don't have to beat people up." Although, those boys had certainly deserved it. She caressed over his chest and down his abdomen, tucking the pads of her fingers into each hard ridge. She purred.

He tangled his fingers in her hair and twisted, forcing her to meet his gaze. "No more casually walking into traps. In fact, no more traps. If there's a trap, you find a way to *not* be in the middle of it."

Well, he'd probably need some time to really figure out the immortal world. Half the fun of traps was springing them. She leaned up and licked along his too firm bottom lip.

His hands—both hands—manacled her hips and lifted her. Fast. Way faster than she could move. He pressed her back to the wall and leaned in, his nose touching hers. Those eyes, blue and dangerous and slightly amused. Yeah, he knew her. Somehow. Maybe this had been his trap all along. "Panties off," he ordered, kissing her before she could respond.

Heck, yeah. She shoved them down, tucking her hands in his jeans and pushing. "Now."

He pushed inside her, going slow, easily holding her, his body warm and strong. "You merely like me?"

Pleasure rippled through her, so much and so strong. She laughed, enjoying everything about him. He was more than she could've ever wanted—and she gave herself over. Finally. "All right. I love you. Happy now?"

"Oh, I'm just getting started." He moved then, driving inside her, taking everything she was. "I think you knew exactly who I'd be. Who I am."

Maybe. Although admitting that to herself hadn't been easy. She'd been alone for so long, and now she'd found somebody who'd never let her go. Yeah, it was a dream she'd always held but hadn't thought would work out. So much for handling him. "Harder."

He went harder, his hands digging into her butt. The ripples were fast, the tide strong. She broke, the room flashing hot, the orgasm stealing her thoughts.

Dropping his head to her neck, he shuddered with his own release. "I love you, too." Then he lifted his head, his gaze bright. "That's fast, right?"

She laughed, happy and not alone. Not even close. "That's immortality, Detective." The faded mark on her palm tingled. "Or maybe it's fate. Does it matter?"

"No." He kissed her deep. "So long as it's forever."

Chapter 16

Epilogue

Tabi snuggled into Evan's side as Dr. Mariana Lopez handed out cake. She took a piece and then handed one to her mate. Her stubborn, sexy, more than she could've ever imagined, mate.

"You took the one that has more frosting," he said, his lips at her ear.

She laughed. He'd given her video to her earlier, and they'd smashed it together. She smiled at Abby sitting next to Noah, trying to steal a frosting flower from him. Cocking her head, she watched Raine Maxwell refuse a piece of cake, his gaze on the shrink.

Mariana sat and smiled. "You've all graduated, and I'm so proud of you."

Tabi took another bite of cake. "You're a good counselor."

"Thanks, but I'm heading back to working with kids. No offense, but adults are too much work." Mariana took a sip of the punch and then frowned. "Who spiked this?"

"I did," Raine said. "Thought we could use something fun." His gaze heated on the woman.

Tabi looked around. "The sheriff's moronic kid hasn't been back in weeks. He doesn't graduate, does he?"

"No," Mariana said, crossing her legs. "I already let the court know, but we'll see what happens."

Evan set his cake aside and reached for the punch. Obviously the alcohol interested him.

Tabi finished her extra frosting, her heart warm. "Evan's running for sheriff. We need a committee, if you're interested."

Raine's eyebrows rose. "You're staying in town?"

"For a while," Tabi confirmed. At least fifty years, but then they'd have to go. "We're rebuilding my factory that somehow caught on fire, and Evan wants to clean up the town. So we're here for now. You?"

"I have a mission and am leaving tonight," Raine affirmed.

Well. So much for Raine and the shrink. The woman was enhanced, somehow, but Tabi didn't know with what. Probably empathy since she had become a psychiatrist. She could've sworn Raine had seemed interested. Too bad.

Mariana looked up at Raine, her expression inscrutable. "There's still an open homicide case, and I think all the witnesses, meaning everyone in this room, has to stay available."

He smiled then, and the sight looked like a warning. "Oh, I'll be back, Mariana. Probably sooner than you'd like."

Tabi swallowed. All righty, then.

Noah finally gave his frosted flower to Abby. "We're staying a while as well. Abby wants to help rebuild the factory, and she likes working with Tabi." He grinned. "If you become sheriff, you'll need a deputy. I'd like to help clean up this town, too. I guess doing it by running for office isn't a bad way."

Tabi smiled. No doubt, Noah had just planned to rip off the sheriff's head, since he'd threatened Abby. This was a better way to go. Two immortals in small town law enforcement. Life was weird. "That's true."

Evan nodded. "I'd like that." He leaned down and kissed her cheek. "See? That's a good plan."

Yeah, probably better than what she'd had in mind for the sheriff. "All right, handsome. We'll try it your way." She leaned up and kissed him, sighing when he took over. So long as they were together.

He leaned back and smiled. "Forever."

* * * *

Also from 1001 Dark Nights and Rebecca Zanetti, discover Vengeance, Blaze Erupting, Tangled, Teased, and Tricked.

* * * *

Coming April 13, 2021 from 1001 Dark Nights and Rebecca Zanetti, a new novella in her Dark Protectors/Rebels series...

Vampire

Dr. Mariana Lopez has finally stopped bailing friends out of difficult situations. Well, except for substituting as the leader for another anger management group, pitching in as a campaign strategist for a prospective sheriff, and babysitting three dogs. Even with such a full life, she can feel the danger around her—a sense that something isn't right. Nightmares harass her, until the real thing comes to life, and only the dark and sexy male sitting in her group can save her. However, with safety comes a price she might not be willing to pay.

Raine Maxwell is one of the Maxwells out of Montana, which means he's not only one of the most deadly vampires alive, but his path is set and his mate has been chosen for him. To save him—to continue his line. Unfortunately, his mate is an enhanced human female who has no idea of her abilities, of his species, or of her future. He'd like to lead her gently into this new world, but his people aren't the only ones who've found her, which puts her into more danger than she can imagine. Plus, in order to follow his laws, he only has one week to convince her that immortality with him is what she wants—and needs.

Sign up for the 1001 Dark Nights Newsletter
and be entered to win a Tiffany Key necklace.

There's a contest every month!

Go to www.1001DarkNights.com to subscribe.

**As a bonus, all subscribers can download
FIVE FREE exclusive books!**

Discover 1001 Dark Nights Collection Seven

Go to www.1001DarkNights.com for more information.

THE BISHOP by Skye Warren
A Tanglewood Novella

TAKEN WITH YOU by Carrie Ann Ryan
A Fractured Connections Novella

DRAGON LOST by Donna Grant
A Dark Kings Novella

SEXY LOVE by Carly Phillips
A Sexy Series Novella

PROVOKE by Rachel Van Dyken
A Seaside Pictures Novella

RAFE by Sawyer Bennett
An Arizona Vengeance Novella

THE NAUGHTY PRINCESS by Claire Contreras
A Sexy Royals Novella

THE GRAVEYARD SHIFT by Darynda Jones
A Charley Davidson Novella

CHARMED by Lexi Blake
A Masters and Mercenaries Novella

SACRIFICE OF DARKNESS by Alexandra Ivy
A Guardians of Eternity Novella

THE QUEEN by Jen Armentrout
A Wicked Novella

BEGIN AGAIN by Jennifer Probst
A Stay Novella

VIXEN by Rebecca Zanetti
A Dark Protectors/Rebels Novella

SLASH by Laurelin Paige
A Slay Series Novella

THE DEAD HEAT OF SUMMER by Heather Graham
A Krewe of Hunters Novella

WILD FIRE by Kristen Ashley
A Chaos Novella

MORE THAN PROTECT YOU by Shayla Black
A More Than Words Novella

LOVE SONG by Kylie Scott
A Stage Dive Novella

CHERISH ME by J. Kenner
A Stark Ever After Novella

SHINE WITH ME by Kristen Proby
A With Me in Seattle Novella

And new from Blue Box Press:

TEASE ME by J. Kenner
A Stark International Novel

FROM BLOOD AND ASH by Jennifer L. Armentrout
A Blood and Ash Novel

QUEEN MOVE by Kennedy Ryan

THE HOUSE OF LONG AGO by Steve Berry and MJ Rose
A Cassiopeia Vitt Adventure

THE BUTTERFLY ROOM by Lucinda Riley

A KINGDOM OF FLESH AND FIRE by Jennifer L. Armentrout
A Blood and Ash Novel

Discover More Rebecca Zanetti

Vengeance
A Dark Protectors/Rebels Novella

Vengeance and revenge are the only forces driving vampire soldier Noah Siosal since losing his brother to an enemy he's been unable to find. He's searched every corner of the globe, going through adversaries and piling up bodies until finally getting a lead. The last place he wants to be is in a ridiculous anger management group with people expressing feelings instead of taking action. Until one fragile human, a green-eyed sweetheart being stalked by danger, catches his eye. One touch, and he realizes vengeance can't be anywhere near her.

Anger and self-preservation are the only motivations Abby Miller needs or wants right now. Falsely accused of attacking the man who's terrorized her for years, she's forced as a plea bargain to attend an anger management counseling group with people with some serious rage issues, while learning true self defense on the side. Yet a man, one more primal than any she's ever met, draws her in a way and into a world deadlier than she's ever imagined. He offers her protection, but she finds the fight is really for his heart, and she's ready to battle.

* * * *

Blaze Erupting
Scorpius Syndrome/A Brigade Novella

Hugh Johnson is nobody's hero, and the idea of being in the limelight makes him want to growl. He takes care of his brothers, does his job, and enjoys a mellow evening hanging with his hound dog and watching the sports channel. So when sweet and sexy Ellie Smithers from his college chemistry class asks him to save millions of people from a nuclear meltdown, he doggedly steps forward while telling himself that the world hasn't changed and he can go back to his relaxing life. One look at Ellie and excitement doesn't seem so bad.

Eleanor Smithers knows that the Scorpius bacteria has and will change life as we know it, but that's a concern for another day. She's been hand-picked as the computer guru for The Brigade, which is the USA's first line of defense against all things Scorpius, including homegrown terrorists who've just been waiting for a chance to strike. Their target is a nuclear power plant in the east, and the only person who can help her is Hugh, the sexy, laconic, dangerous man she had a crush on so long ago.

* * * *

Tangled
A Dark Protectors—Reece Family Novella

Now that her mask has finally slipped…

Ginny O'Toole has spent a lifetime repaying her family's debt, and she's finally at the end of her servitude with one last job. Of course, it couldn't be easy. After stealing the computer files that will free her once and for all, she finds herself on the run from a pissed off vampire who has never fallen for her helpless act. A deadly predator too sexy for his own good. If he doesn't knock it off, he's going to see just how powerful she can really be.

He won't be satisfied until she's completely bare.

Theo Reese had been more than irritated at the beautiful yet helpless witch he'd known a century ago, thinking she was just useless fluff who enjoyed messing with men's heads. The second he discovers she's a ruthless thief determined to bring down his family, his blood burns and his interest peaks, sending his true nature into hunting mode. When he finds her, and he will, she'll understand the real meaning of helpless.

* * * *

Tricked
A Dark Protectors—Reese Family Novella

He Might Save Her

Former police psychologist Ronni Alexander had it all before a poison attacked her heart and gave her a death sentence. Now, on her last leg, she has an opportunity to live if she mates a vampire. A real vampire. One night of sex and a good bite, and she'd live forever with no more weaknesses. Well, except for the vampire whose dominance is over the top, and who has no clue how to deal with a modern woman who can take care of herself.

She Might Kill Him

Jared Reese, who has no intention of ever mating for anything other than convenience, agrees to help out his new sister in law by saving her friend's life with a quick tussle in bed. The plan seems so simple. They'd mate, and he move on with his life and take risks as a modern pirate should. Except after one night with Ronni, one moment of her sighing his name, and he wants more than a mating of convenience. Now all he has to do is convince Ronni she wants the same thing. Good thing he's up for a good battle.

* * * *

Teased
A Dark Protectors—Reece Family Novella

The Hunter

For almost a century, the Realm's most deadly assassin, Chalton Reese, has left war and death in the past, turning instead to strategy, reason, and technology. His fingers, still stained with blood, now protect with a keyboard instead of a weapon. Until the vampire king sends him on one more mission; to hunt down a human female with the knowledge to destroy the Realm. A woman with eyes like emeralds, a brain to match his own, and a passion that might destroy them both—if the enemy on their heels doesn't do so first.

The Hunted

Olivia Roberts has foregone relationships with wimpy metro-sexuals in favor of pursuing a good story, bound and determined to uncover the truth, any truth. When her instincts start humming about missing proprietary information, she has no idea her search for a story will lead her to a ripped, sexy, and dangerous male beyond any human man. Setting aside the unbelievable fact that he's a vampire and she's his prey, she discovers that trusting him is the only chance they have to survive the danger stalking them both.

Disorderly Conduct
The Anna Albertini Files Book 1
By Rebecca Zanetti

A fun, sexy, suspenseful new series from New York Times Bestselling Author Rebecca Zanetti! Meet Anna Albertini!

Bullets and Kisses Can Burn

The last person Anna Albertini expects to see in an orange jumpsuit in District Court—a place she SO doesn't belong as a new prosecuting attorney—is Aiden Devlin, the man who'd saved her life when they were kids. For years, she has dreamed about him. Now here he is—his eyes blue, his chest wide, and his hands in cuffs.

Sure, Aiden says he doesn't want her help, and his ties to a deadly motorcycle club should give her warning. Yes, her new boss is a sexy Italian bad boy who might be using the case to climb to the top. Plus, the detective assigned to the case, with his green eyes and broad shoulders, wants her to stay out of his way.

With so much testosterone surrounding her all of a sudden, most women would find it hard to concentrate. This might be why the case leads Anna to yelp during a spa appointment, fall out of a tree, and chase a naked old man around the courtroom. It's a good thing Anna learned a long time ago to be her own hero, no matter how fast the bullets fly or the kisses consume.

* * * *

Excerpt:
Ducking my head, I took a sharp right, hit the end of the street, and turned for the courthouse. The building had been erected when the timber companies and the mines had been prosperous in the area and was made of deep mahogany and real marble brought in from Italy. Instead of walking downstairs like I had the last two weeks, I climbed up a floor to the district court level. It even smelled different than the lower floors. More like lemon polish and something serious. Oh yeah. Life and

death and felonies. My knees wobbled, so I straightened my blue pencil skirt and did a quick check of my white blouse to make sure I hadn't pitted out.

Nope. Good. I shouldn't be too scared, because the pseudo-metropolis of Timber City had only 49,000 residents, roughly the same as a large state college. But compared to my hometown of Silverville, which was about fifty miles east through a mountain pass, this was the big city.

My wedges squeaked on the gleaming floor. I pushed open the heavy door and made my way past the pews to the desk to the right, facing the judge's tall bench. My temples started to thrum. I remained standing at the table and set down the case files before flipping open the first one.

A commotion sounded, and two men strode in from the back, both wearing fancy gray suits. I recognized the first man, and an odd relief took me again, even though he was clearly there as the defendant's attorney and on the opposite side of the aisle as me. "Mr. O'Malley," I murmured.

He held out his hand. "Call me Chuck, Anna." He was a fishing buddy of my dad's and had been for years. "They've thrown you into District Court already?"

I shifted my feet. "It's a long story." That would be public shortly. "The DEA took Scot away in handcuffs," I said.

Chuck straightened, his gray eyebrows shooting up. "Charges?"

"The warrant said something about narcotics." We were on different sides right now, and Chuck was a phenomenal criminal defense attorney, but the truth was the truth and would be out anyway. "He probably needs a good lawyer."

"I'll check it out after this hearing." Chuck's eyes gleamed the same way they did when my Nonna Albertini brought her apple pie to a community picnic. He nodded at his client, a guy in his late twenties with a trimmed goatee and thinning hair. "This is Ralph Ceranio. He's pleading not guilty today."

Thank goodness. That just meant we would set things for trial.

Chuck smiled. "Unless you agree to dismiss."

I smiled back. "I'd like to keep my job for another week." Probably. "So no."

Chuck turned as the bailiff entered through a side door by the bench and told everyone to stand, even though we were already standing. Then Judge Hallenback swept in.

Oh my. My mouth dropped open, and I quickly snapped it shut. It was rumored the judge had been going downhill for some time, and I was thinking that for once, rumors were right. While he had to only be in his mid-sixties, maybe he had early dementia? Today he wore a customary black robe with a charming red bow tie visible above the fold. It contrasted oddly with the bright purple hat with tassels hanging down on top of his head. A bunch of colorful drawn dots covered his left hand while a gray and white striped kitten was cradled in his right, and he hummed the anthem to *Baby Got Back* as he walked.

He set the cat down and banged his gavel, opening a manila file already on his desk. "Elk County vs Ralph Ceranio for felony counts of fraud, theft, and burglary."

I swallowed.

"My client pleads not guilty and requests a jury trial, your honor," Chuck said, concern glowing in his eyes. He and the judge had probably been friends for years, too.

"Bail?" the judge asked, yanking open his robe to reveal a Hallenback's Used Car Lot T-shirt. Oh yeah. The judge and his brother owned a couple of car dealerships in the area. If he retired now, he'd be just fine. "Hello? Prosecuting attorney talk now," he muttered.

I quickly read Scot's notes. "Two hundred thousand dollars. The defendant is a flight risk, your honor. He has access to a private plane and several vehicles."

"Everyone has a private plane. Heck. I even have one." The judge shook his head before Chuck could respond. "Fifty thousand dollars. How many days do you need for trial?"

I had no clue. I didn't even know the case.

"Probably a week, Judge," Chuck said, helping me out.

I could only nod.

"All right." The judge reached for a calendar and announced the date six months away. "See ya then."

Chuck patted my shoulder. "I'll be in touch."

I swallowed again, wanting to beg him to stay with me for the second hearing. But I had to at least act like I had a clue what I was doing. The bailiff, a brawny guy whose nightstick somehow looked thicker than usual, moved for the door he'd emerged from earlier and opened it. He grabbed an arm covered by an orange jumper while I shuffled the files and looked down, trying to read Scot's mangled notes.

Hopefully I could get caught up quickly.

The judge slammed down his gavel again. "Elk County vs. Aiden Devlin for narcotics possession and intent to distribute."

I stilled. Everything inside me, from thoughts to feelings to dreams and hard reality, just halted. I slowly turned to face a tall man dressed in an orange jumpsuit. Oh my God. "Aiden," I whispered, the entire world grinding to a harsh stop.

He smiled, his eyes bluer than I remembered, his face much more rugged. "Hi, angel."

Guardian's Grace
Dark Protectors Book 12
By Rebecca Zanetti

Want to see more of Adare and his wayward mate? Take a sneak peek at Guardian's Grace:

Duty—or desire?

Vampire soldier Adare O'Cearbhaill's default setting is cranky. Or irritated. Or down-right hostile. Still, as a Highlander of honor and duty, he stepped up to save an enhanced and special human female by mating her—with merely a bite and a brand. The last person he wants in his life is a fragile human, yet he can't get her out of his mind as she regains her strength before taking off for parts unknown. And when he discovers she is in danger, nothing can stop him from hunting her down—whether she likes it or not.

There's only one way to find out...

Photographer Grace Cooper has had it with vampires, demons, and the rest of an immortal world she was happier not knowing about. She also doesn't believe she's destined for some great battle because of an old birthmark. Forget the fact that her mate is the sexiest thing on two stubborn feet, or that her brand is fading along with her health. She'll handle things on her own—until an old enemy reappears and she learns the only way to stay alive is to *actually* mate, wild sex and all, with that ripped and dangerous Adare—a powerful, captivating Highlander who demands nothing less than everything...

* * * *

Excerpt:
Adare's nostrils flared, and Grace's body reacted, stopping her in her tracks. Then he started moving toward her, smooth and graceful, his six-foot-six height and broad chest making him look like the proverbial immovable object.

Sebastian swallowed loudly and backed to her side. "That guy is huge. Like huge huge." He looked toward her, one fluorescent blue contact falling out of his eye. "What have you gotten me into?"

The lump in her throat nearly choked her. "Nothing. You're fine, but don't go around pretending to be something you're not. Trust me, Sebastian."

"Freddy," the kid croaked. "My name is Freddy. Not Sebastian. I thought that sounded more like a creature of the night."

The huge blond guy's mouth dropped open and then shut quickly.

Oh, this was so bad. She'd tried hard not to leave a trail. Fake name, fake email address, and she'd even moved around to use different library computers and IP addresses—in different towns. What kind of laws had she broken? As far as she knew, there weren't prisons for immortals, so what did that leave? Death for treason?

Not that she wasn't dying anyway.

The blond, his black eyes taking in the entire room, quickly stepped up to the bar and flashed a badge. "U.S. Government. We only want those two for federal crimes."

"Whew," one of the kids in the back sighed.

The bartender shrugged, still drying off a beer glass with a dirty towel. "Take 'em."

Freddy lifted his hands. "I haven't done anything. Really. The chick is nuts. She thought I was a vampire, and she wanted to buy blood, so I figured, why not? Freaky sex might be fun."

"Shut. Up." Adare manacled Freddy's neck with one hand, cutting off all sound. Without taking his gaze off Grace, he flicked his wrist and tossed Freddy toward the blond. "Nick? Take him, please."

The *please*, for some reason, sent shivers down Grace's back. Her legs weakened, but she lifted her chin, facing Adare. It had been nearly three years since they'd crossed paths, and he appeared even better-looking than she remembered. Meaner and bigger, too. A pissed-off expression on him was normal, but this one was new. All heat and fury. "I'll get going, too," she said, taking another step back.

Nick caught Freddy and leaned to the side, holding the human like a rag doll. "Adare? Do you know this female?"

Adare slowly nodded, his focus stronger than any hold. "She's my mate."

"I am not," she retorted.

"Yes. You. Are." Adare's face was as impenetrable as rock, even as the words rolled out with that brogue.

Nick's light eyebrows rose. He looked around the bar and, apparently satisfied that nobody was going to attack, returned his focus to Adare. "What's your mate doing trying to buy vampire blood in Colorado?" he whispered.

It sounded ridiculous. Heat spread up Grace's chest to her face, causing her cheeks to pound.

Adare's gaze followed the heat, making her even warmer. "We're about to get an answer to that question." He held out one broad hand, no leniency on his hard face. "Let's do this somewhere else."

It was an order, not a question.

"No." She said it softly but with authority. The bond of their mating was almost gone, and he had no hold on her. He never would, which suited them both just fine. "This was obviously a mistake, so let's just go our separate ways."

His lids half-lowered, slowly and deliberately, the deadly predator at his core fully visible. Not many people disobeyed the dangerous hybrid, and a human female, one whose life he had saved, shouldn't even have thought about it. But she was no longer his responsibility, and she was done being lost.

"Grace." One word, said in that brogue, with a demand that was absolute.

If she could run, she would. Instead, her body froze, her heart thundering. "I know I goofed up here, and I won't do it again." The appeasing note in her voice ticked her off, but she wasn't up to a physical struggle right now. This disastrous meeting had taken weeks to set up. "Let's just forget this and move on."

"Have you lost your mind?" He sounded more curious than angry.

Hope flared through her. "Yes, briefly. It happens." He'd never wanted anything to do with her, so giving him an out should work nicely. A simple apology—she tried to sound sincere—although she wanted to kick him in the shin instead. He'd always been a jackass, but there was no doubt he'd win any physical fight. Even at her best, which she wasn't close to right now, she couldn't take him. It was doubtful anybody could. "This whole thing was a mistake, and I'm sorry." She choked on the last word.

"Let's go." His hand was still out.

An electric shiver took her. "Adare, I don't think—"

"Exactly. You didn't think." A muscle ticked in his rugged jaw, revealing the effort his control was costing him. "Apparently that's something we need to discuss. At length."

Was that a threat? Yep. That was definitely a threat. "Not a chance," she snapped, drawing on anger to camouflage panic.

Nick turned Freddy and shoved him toward the door. "We need to take this somewhere else," he muttered.

"Not me," Freddy said. "Really. This isn't my fault." He pushed back against Nick, his voice dropping to a whine. "I just wanted to get laid. Whatever she's into, I'm not a part of it. Please. Let me go."

Nick opened the door and propelled him into the snowstorm. The wind shrieked, blowing snow inside.

Adare grasped her upper arm. "Now."

She tugged free. "Absolutely not."

"I wasn't asking." For a big male, he moved surprisingly fast. He ducked his head, and within a heartbeat, she was over his shoulder, heading toward the door.

Her chin hit his lower back, and her stomach lurched, the alcohol she'd consumed stirring around. She pounded against his waist with her good hand, not close to stopping him. This was a disaster. Panic grabbed her, and she tried to struggle but could barely move. "Let me go. Now."

"Hold on to your strength, Grace. You're going to need it." With that, he took her into the storm.

About Rebecca Zanetti

New York Times and *USA Today bestselling* author Rebecca Zanetti has published more than fifty novels, which have been translated into several languages, with millions of copies sold world-wide. Her books have received Publisher's Weekly starred reviews, won RT Reviewer Choice awards, and have been featured in Entertainment Weekly, Woman's World, and Women's Day Magazines. Her novels have also been included in Amazon best books of the year and have been favorably reviewed in both the Washington Post and the New York Times Book Reviews. Rebecca has ridden in a locked Chevy trunk, has asked the unfortunate UPS guy to release her from a set of handcuffs, and has discovered the best silver mine shafts in which to bury a body...all in the name of research. Honest. Find Rebecca at: www.RebeccaZanetti.com

Discover 1001 Dark Nights

COLLECTION ONE
FOREVER WICKED by Shayla Black
CRIMSON TWILIGHT by Heather Graham
CAPTURED IN SURRENDER by Liliana Hart
SILENT BITE: A SCANGUARDS WEDDING by Tina Folsom
DUNGEON GAMES by Lexi Blake
AZAGOTH by Larissa Ione
NEED YOU NOW by Lisa Renee Jones
SHOW ME, BABY by Cherise Sinclair
ROPED IN by Lorelei James
TEMPTED BY MIDNIGHT by Lara Adrian
THE FLAME by Christopher Rice
CARESS OF DARKNESS by Julie Kenner

COLLECTION TWO
WICKED WOLF by Carrie Ann Ryan
WHEN IRISH EYES ARE HAUNTING by Heather Graham
EASY WITH YOU by Kristen Proby
MASTER OF FREEDOM by Cherise Sinclair
CARESS OF PLEASURE by Julie Kenner
ADORED by Lexi Blake
HADES by Larissa Ione
RAVAGED by Elisabeth Naughton
DREAM OF YOU by Jennifer L. Armentrout
STRIPPED DOWN by Lorelei James
RAGE/KILLIAN by Alexandra Ivy/Laura Wright
DRAGON KING by Donna Grant
PURE WICKED by Shayla Black
HARD AS STEEL by Laura Kaye
STROKE OF MIDNIGHT by Lara Adrian
ALL HALLOWS EVE by Heather Graham
KISS THE FLAME by Christopher Rice
DARING HER LOVE by Melissa Foster
TEASED by Rebecca Zanetti
THE PROMISE OF SURRENDER by Liliana Hart

TAKE THE BRIDE by Carly Phillips
INDULGE ME by J. Kenner
THE KING by Jennifer L. Armentrout
QUIET MAN by Kristen Ashley
ABANDON by Rachel Van Dyken
THE OPEN DOOR by Laurelin Paige
CLOSER by Kylie Scott
SOMETHING JUST LIKE THIS by Jennifer Probst
BLOOD NIGHT by Heather Graham
TWIST OF FATE by Jill Shalvis
MORE THAN PLEASURE YOU by Shayla Black
WONDER WITH ME by Kristen Proby
THE DARKEST ASSASSIN by Gena Showalter

Discover Blue Box Press

TAME ME by J. Kenner
TEMPT ME by J. Kenner
DAMIEN by J. Kenner
TEASE ME by J. Kenner
REAPER by Larissa Ione
THE SURRENDER GATE by Christopher Rice
SERVICING THE TARGET by Cherise Sinclair
THE LAKE OF LEARNING by Steve Berry and MJ Rose
THE MUSEUM OF MYSTERIES by Steve Berry and MJ Rose

On Behalf of 1001 Dark Nights,

Liz Berry, M.J. Rose, and Jillian Stein would like to thank ~

Steve Berry
Doug Scofield
Benjamin Stein
Kim Guidroz
Social Butterfly PR
Asha Hossain
Chris Graham
Chelle Olson
Kasi Alexander
Jessica Johns
Dylan Stockton
Richard Blake
and Simon Lipskar

Made in the USA
San Bernardino, CA
12 August 2020